The Rocky Road to Revenge

The chairlift moved down the mountain, then stopped. Joe and Terry waited, but the chair didn't start up again. Joe spotted a cable pole with a ladder leading to the ground.

"I'm climbing down," Joe said.

"Forget it," Terry said. "If you fall, we'll be worse off than we are now."

Joe figured there was about a three-story drop from the chair to the ground but that he had a good chance to make it to the pole.

He stepped on the seat and grabbed hold of a metal bar above his head. The chair rocked slightly. Joe placed a foot on the safety bar, tested it, then put his other foot on the bar.

Keeping one hand on the bar above him, he reached with the other for the ladder. His fingers were a few inches short of their target. Joe shifted his weight onto one leg, sent the other back for balance, and stretched his arm out farther.

Suddenly the chair began to move down the mountain again.

A lightning bolt of fear pulsed through Joe's body as he toppled forward and found himself falling!

The Hardy Boys
Mystery Stories

Available from MINSTREL Books

THE HARDY BOYS®

151

THE ROCKY ROAD TO REVENGE

FRANKLIN W. DIXON

A MINSTREL® BOOK

Published by POCKET BOOKS
New York London Toronto Sydney Tokyo Singapore

A MINSTREL PAPERBACK *Original*

A Minstrel Book published by
POCKET BOOKS, a division of Simon & Schuster Inc.
1230 Avenue of the Americas, New York, NY 10020

Front cover illustration by John Youssi

Produced by Mega-Books, Inc.

ISBN: 0-671-02172-9

First Minstrel Books printing August 1998

10 9 8 7 6 5 4 3 2 1

Printed in the U.S.A.

Contents

THE ROCKY ROAD TO REVENGE

1 Out of the Sky

The iron horseshoe twirled wildly through the air, then landed on the ground with a thump.

"I think the idea is to get the shoe in the box of sand, not the next county," Frank Hardy told his brother, Joe.

Joe walked over to retrieve his two misfired horseshoes. "Hey, give me a break," he said. "I have to get used to this altitude."

Earlier that afternoon Joe and Frank had arrived high in the Rocky Mountains of Colorado. Now majestic peaks soared upward in every direction, their shapes darkening with the setting sun.

"No fighting, boys," Terry Taylor called out. With her sun-streaked brown hair and deeply

1

tanned skin, Terry looked as if she spent more time outdoors than in.

Terry was one of Joe and Frank's friends from Bayport High. She was spending the summer working at Silver Crest, a small resort village, and had invited the Hardys to come visit for a week. The resort specialized in rafting, fishing, and biking expeditions. Terry was one of the rafting guides, and she also helped out with the general running of the place.

"Ah, breathe that air," Frank said as he lined up his next shot. "It's so fresh at this altitude."

"Stop stalling and shoot," Joe said with mock impatience.

Frank took careful aim with the horseshoe, his eyes fixed on the iron bar rising out of the box of sand. At eighteen, Frank was tall, with dark brown hair and dark eyes. He had a sharp, methodical mind that he applied to everything he did, whether it was schoolwork, catching villains, or playing a game of horseshoes.

Frank sent the horseshoe sailing through the air. It hit the iron bar with a clang and rested up against it.

"A leaner," Frank said. "That gives me three more points. Which means I win the game twenty-one to, uh . . . three."

"Congratulations," Joe said with a hint of annoyance in his voice. Blond-haired Joe was a year younger and an inch shorter than Frank. He

2

didn't enjoy being beaten by his brother at anything. Joe was also intelligent, but more often than not his actions were guided by his emotions rather than his brain.

Frank and Joe handed their horseshoes to a man and his young son, who were waiting to play. The Hardys walked with Terry to a two-story wooden building that looked like something out of the Old West. A hanging sign announced that it was the Silver Crest HQ. Terry said that this was the resort's headquarters, with a check-in area, mess hall, supply shop, offices, and dorm rooms for the employees.

Terry waved to three women who were sitting in comfortable chairs on the front porch.

"Those women are sisters from Texas," she said to Frank and Joe. "They've been coming here since they were girls."

"And those two," Terry said, pointing to a man and a woman rocking in a swing suspended between two trees, "are a stockbroker and his wife. They're newlyweds from New York City. They're here on their honeymoon."

Joe knew Colorado was one of the great vacation spots, drawing people from all over the world with its beautiful scenery and year-round recreational opportunities.

"Is everyone having a good time?" a man said as he stepped out of the HQ. He was a big man in his forties with reddish hair and a beard. He wore a denim jacket and cowboy boots, and sported a turquoise ring on his little finger.

"Wouldn't want to be anywhere else," Joe said.

"This is Clay Robinson," Terry said. "He's the owner of Silver Crest. Mr. Robinson, these are the friends I was telling you about, Frank and Joe Hardy."

"It's a pleasure to meet you," Robinson said, giving each boy a hearty handshake.

"Same here," Frank replied.

Robinson stuck two fingers in his mouth and gave a loud whistle. A white, medium-size dog trotted over. She looked up at Robinson with eager brown eyes.

"Meet my dog, Stella," Robinson said proudly.

"What kind is she?" Joe asked. He knelt to pet the dog's sleek white coat.

"Part terrier, part retriever, and all heart," Robinson said with a chuckle.

"This sure is a great place you've got here," Frank told Robinson.

"Why, thank you," Robinson said. "And it's about to get even better."

"How do you mean?" Frank asked.

"Come on, I'll show you," Robinson said. Frank, Joe, and Stella followed Robinson across the Silver Crest grounds. Terry remained at the HQ. They passed a picnic area, a volleyball court, tennis courts, and a cluster of log cabins where the guests stayed.

4

"This whole area for about fifty square miles is known as Moondance Pass," Robinson said as they walked. "It's got some of the most beautiful scenery in the state and some of the best ski slopes you could ever break a leg on. Right now there're only a few small resorts, like this one, around here. But I'm about to bring the world to Moondance Pass on a large scale."

Robinson stopped at the edge of the grounds. A construction site stood a quarter mile away, at a lower elevation. Frank could see a large, half-finished structure surrounded by trucks, tractors, and about a dozen construction workers. The construction area was illuminated by several large spotlights.

"I'm in the process of building a hotel and condominium complex there," Robinson said. "It'll be a first-class establishment. I'm calling it the Golden Dream. See," he said, pointing to a huge mountain behind the site, "it's right at the base of the mountain. You'll be able to ski practically to your front door."

"When do you expect it to be ready?" Frank asked.

"I'm hoping to have a portion of it open by ski season," Robinson said. "As you can see, I've got crews working into the night. The whole complex should be ready by next summer, and if that goes well, I've got plenty of room to expand."

"The Golden Dream ought to be a gold mine

for you," Joe said. "I'm surprised no one has built something like it around here before."

Joe noticed that Robinson was looking at the construction site with the pride a father reserves for admiring his child.

"Well, it hasn't been easy," Robinson said. "There was resistance from the locals. But when Clay Robinson gets it into his head to do something, by golly, he does it. Always remember that, boys. Stick to your guns, no matter what."

"Good advice," Frank commented.

Stella began rubbing her head against Joe's leg. "Come on, I'll race you back to the HQ," Joe told the dog.

Joe took off with Stella galloping beside him. Joe was breathing hard by the time he reached the HQ, but Stella looked as if she was just getting warmed up.

"That's it for now," Joe said. "I'm supposed to be on vacation, you know." Joe sat on the ground to catch his breath, and Stella lay faithfully beside him.

Joe spent a few moments watching the night settle in. The sky was darkening into a canvas of deep black, against which the stars glittered like tiny diamonds. The night was so clear that Joe could make out pearly textures in the nearly full moon.

"Yeah, this is the life," Joe said to Stella. Everything was still except for a slight breeze in the trees and the three women from Texas chatting on the porch. Joe zipped up his jacket. The mountain air had turned chilly, but Joe was thinking it might be nice to sleep outside under the stars.

Just then Stella jumped up and began to run back and forth, barking loudly. Joe recognized it as the kind of bark a dog makes when a stranger sets foot on its property.

"What is it, girl?" Joe asked. He noticed the dog was looking at the sky. Joe glanced up. Then he sprang to his feet, his blue eyes greeted by an amazing sight.

A vaporous cloudlike formation hovered in the sky. It was not a cloud. The shape of the formation shifted, now almost billowing like a sheet blowing in the wind. And most striking of all, the thing glowed a dark shade of orange. The color reminded Joe of a Halloween pumpkin.

Joe saw Frank and Robinson approaching as Terry stepped outside. "Hey, guys, take a look at this!" Joe called out.

All three looked up. Joe saw the shock on their faces. Other resort guests had gathered and were also looking up at the sky in amazement.

"Wow!" Terry exclaimed. "This is incredible!"

"You can say that again," Frank said.

"In all my days," one of the women from Texas said, "I swear I've never seen anything like it."

Joe realized that Stella's barking had stopped.

He saw that Robinson was kneeling beside the dog, calming her with even strokes. Robinson and Stella were both watching the glow.

Joe looked up at the sky again. The orange formation was moving across the sky, but it was too far away for Joe to determine its speed. Then he noticed something hovering in the center of the formation. It was a tiny spot of intense white light.

The Japanese man called to the others. "Could this be what you call a spy airplane?"

"If that's an airplane," one of the Texas women called, "I'll eat a plate of my horse's hay. There're no airplanes like that anywhere I've seen."

"Perhaps it's the aurora borealis," the stockbroker suggested. "You know, those lights that flash in the sky."

"I've never heard of the northern lights being visible around here," Robinson pointed out.

"Well, it sure has to be something!" Frank said.

Joe Hardy had seen a lot of bizarre things in his seventeen years, but nothing quite like this. "I can't believe I'm saying this," he told the others, "but I think we're witnessing a genuine UFO."

2 The Talk of the Town

As everyone watched, the strange orange formation grew dimmer and dimmer. Then, as quickly as it had appeared, it vanished.

Now there was only the black night sky, the stars, and the moon. Joe noticed that the others were still observing the sky in hushed wonder.

"Where in tarnation did it go?" one of the Texas women asked. "And what in tarnation was it?"

Terry turned to her boss. "Mr. Robinson, what do you think?"

As he ran a hand along his dog's back, Robinson seemed lost in thought. Then he gave a chuckle and said, "Oh, it was mighty strange. I'll

9

admit that. But I'm sure there's a perfectly logical explanation for it."

"I agree," Frank said.

Joe turned to Frank. "What's your explanation?"

"It could have been a comet or a meteor," Frank said.

"That might explain the orange formation," Joe argued, "but I could swear I saw an intense white light moving inside it."

Frank gave a doubtful look. "And I'll bet you also think it's being flown by little green creatures from another planet."

"Hey," Joe told his brother, "it's not impossible!"

"I saw the white light, too," the stockbroker said.

"Well, it could have been what's known as earthlight," Frank said. "I did a huge report on it in school. I know that earthlights are often mistaken for UFOs."

"I guess," Joe said, but he was unconvinced. He felt there had to be something more to this phenomenon.

Everyone spent a few minutes discussing the orange glow. Then Clay Robinson gave Stella a pat and stood up.

"Listen," he told Frank and Joe, "I need to drive into Coalville to sign some papers for my lawyer. It has to do with the construction contracts. I'm going to meet him at his house. Maybe you boys would like a quick look at the town."

"That sounds great," Frank said.

"Why don't you join us, Terry?" Robinson asked.

"Fine with me," Terry said.

Robinson, the Hardys, and Terry piled into Robinson's maroon Jeep, and soon they were winding along Highway 134. Sitting up front, Frank looked out the window at the shadowy shapes of mountains looming in the distance.

"There are two towns in Moondance Pass," Robinson said as he steered around a curve. "Coalville is the larger, and then there's Parnassa a bit farther down the highway. Times have been hard around here since coal mining disappeared, but I'm hoping the Golden Dream will create a lot of jobs."

Frank saw a biker zoom around the side of the Jeep and swerve dangerously close in front of it. "Hey, watch it," Frank called out the window.

"Hang on!" Robinson called. The Jeep jolted as Robinson slammed on the brakes. Another biker immediately swerved in front of the Jeep and stayed just as close as the first.

Frank could see the two bikers in the headlights. They were two young women wearing helmets and biking shorts. The bikers now rode just in front of the Jeep, apparently in no hurry to clear the way. Robinson honked angrily, and the

11

two bikers zoomed ahead, their red taillights getting smaller in the distance.

"They should be more careful," Frank said.

"No, they were just doing that to annoy me," Robinson said as he continued down the highway. "That was Bev and Myra, two employees I had a problem with recently."

"What happened?" Joe asked from the backseat.

There was scorn in Robinson's voice. "I hired them last spring to work at Silver Crest. They did all sorts of things, just like Terry, but their specialty was taking guests on mountain bike expeditions. They were good guides, but they had an attitude problem from the start. Then two weeks ago I discovered they had stolen some things from my office. I fired them, of course, and now they have a grudge against me."

"They're not the nicest girls in the world," Terry said from her seat next to Joe.

"We get a lot of drifters like them," Robinson said. "Young folks who just like living in the mountains and doing odd jobs to get by. They're not ambitious, but most of them don't cause trouble the way those two do."

Before long the highway turned into the main street of a town. "Welcome to Coalville," Robinson announced. "Population: Not very big." Joe looked out the window to see a sleepy-looking downtown area. None of the buildings rose more than three stories, and a few of the older ones had the feel of a bygone mining town.

Robinson stopped in front of a general store that looked about a hundred years old. A wooden sign read, The Black Elk.

"I'll drop you here," Robinson said. "First I'm going to fill up with gas, and then I'm going for the papers. My lawyer, Jim Wilkins, lives over on Waring Road."

Robinson looked at his watch. "It's nine o'clock now. I should be back soon. How about I pick you up right here at nine forty-five?"

"That sounds good," Frank said as he, Joe, and Terry climbed out of the Jeep. "That'll give us some time to walk around."

Frank saw a group of people gathered in front of the store. By their gestures toward the sky, he could tell they were talking about the mysterious orange phenomenon.

An older man was standing near the group, leaning against a timber post. Terry took the Hardys over. "I'd like you to meet Max Jagowitz," she said. "He owns the Black Elk, and he's lived in Moondance Pass all his life."

"All seventy-seven years," Jagowitz said as he vigorously shook hands with Frank.

Frank studied the man. He looked a good fifteen years younger than seventy-seven. Wearing a hunting jacket and baseball cap, the man seemed a model of good health.

"I've lived here all my life all right," Jagowitz said in a gravelly voice. "But that man who dropped you off—Robinson—he's about to ruin the place for my next seventy-seven years."

"Did you see that orange light?" Terry asked quickly. Frank could tell that she was eager to change the subject.

"Sure did," Max answered. "That's what all these people are yapping about. Some of them think it was a crazy ship from outer space."

Joe smiled. "What do you think?"

"I think it's time I got home or my wife will be calling the police," Jagowitz replied with a chuckle. "Evening, all." He tipped his baseball cap, then walked to a beat-up car parked down the street.

Frank noticed a man pass Jagowitz and walk in their direction. "Who's this guy?" Frank asked Terry.

"Oh, he's the local eccentric," Terry said. "His name is Sykes. The reason he's so excited is—"

"Good evening," the man said as he hurried over to the group. "My name is Alastair Sykes. Did you folks happen to witness the celestial phenomenon a little while ago?"

Sykes was tall and unusually slender with wispy hair. But his most striking features, Joe thought, were his intense eyes, magnified by thick glasses.

"Yes, we saw it," Joe answered.

14

"Well, I'm a scientist who specializes in extra-terrestrial communication," Sykes said. "And I have good reason to believe that glow was emanating from a space vehicle."

"So that *was* a UFO we saw?" Joe asked.

"So far no one I've spoken to has been able to identify the phenomenon," Sykes said, "so, yes, at the moment it is a UFO. Now I've got some forms here and I wonder if you could each fill one out. You just write down what you saw and then your name, address, and phone number."

"Why do you want these?" Frank asked.

"To verify the sighting," Sykes said. He pulled some pens and papers from a leather briefcase. "I'm collecting as many eyewitness reports as I can."

"Sure, I'll fill one out," Joe said. "My friends will, too."

Frank, Joe, and Terry each took a form and leaned on a parked car to write. After a few minutes, they handed their forms back to Sykes.

"Many thanks," Sykes said as he stuffed the forms into his briefcase. "Now if you'll excuse me, I have a lot of ground to cover tonight."

Joe opened his mouth to ask Sykes some questions about his work and about the orange glow, but the man was already scurrying away toward his car.

The Hardys and Terry talked with a few other people who were gathered nearby. Frank

15

checked his watch. "It's nine-twenty. We've still got some time," he said. "What else can you show us, Terry?"

"Not much from the inside, since almost everything here closes early, especially on a Wednesday night, but I can walk you around town."

Terry showed the Hardys the city hall and public library, both of which were brick buildings from the 1920s. When the trio returned to the Black Elk at nine forty-five, Robinson had not yet arrived. They passed the time talking for a half-hour. Robinson still did not appear.

Terry checked her watch. "I don't know why he's so late. Waring Road isn't very far from here. Why don't we walk in that direction."

Terry and the Hardys walked out of the downtown area and soon came to a dirt road. The road was dark and quiet, surrounded by the silhouettes of trees, brush, and rocks.

After they had walked for about a quarter of a mile, Joe noticed something up ahead on the road. "Hey, look," he said. "I think that's Robinson's Jeep."

Frank, Joe, and Terry trotted up to the vehicle. Sure enough, it was Robinson's maroon Jeep, parked on the side of the road. The driver-side door was wide open, and the keys were still in the ignition.

"This doesn't look good," Terry said.

"Maybe he had car trouble," Joe said. "He could have gone for help."

Frank glanced up and down the road. "But why would he leave the keys in the ignition and the door wide open? It makes no sense. Let's take a look around."

Frank, Joe, and Terry spent a few minutes searching the area, but they found no sign of Robinson.

"I don't like this," Joe said. "No one leaves a car like this unless something is wrong."

"Mr. Robinson!" Terry called out. "Mr. Robinson! It's me, Terry! Can you hear me?"

There was no answer. Except for a slight rustling in the trees, the area was dead quiet. Joe saw the moon glowing above.

"I don't know what's going on," Frank said quietly, "but I think Clay Robinson is in some kind of trouble. No one just vanishes into thin air."

3 Tombstone Trail

"We should go to the police," Terry said in a shaky voice.

"Definitely," Joe answered as he put a hand on Terry's shoulder.

Frank knew it might help if they could pinpoint the time Robinson had disappeared. He looked at his watch. "It's ten-twenty. Let's check the gas station and Robinson's lawyer's house," he said. "We can see if he made it to either of those places."

All three got into the Jeep. Terry started the engine and drove down the road. Before they had gotten far, the headlights picked up a man walking toward them along the road. "Do you know who that is, Terry?" Frank asked.

"No, I don't," Terry replied.

"Maybe he saw Robinson," Frank said. "Let's ask him."

When Terry reached the man, she stopped the Jeep, and Frank leaned out his window. The man was in his twenties, with shaggy blond hair and ragged clothing. Even though it was night, he wore mirrored sunglasses with a blue tint. Frank guessed he was one of the drifter types Robinson had told them about earlier.

"Excuse me," Frank said. "In the last hour or so did you happen to see a man around here? In his forties, reddish hair, beard."

"Nope," the drifter said with little expression in his voice.

"Did you see anything at all suspicious?" Frank asked. "Like a car speeding by or something?"

"Nope," the man said again.

"Do you need a lift somewhere?" Frank asked.

"Nope," the man said. "Just out for a stroll."

Frank studied the man a moment then said, "Okay, thanks."

"Oh, wait," the man said, holding up a hand. "I did see something strange. There was this really psychedelic light in the sky. Did you see it?"

"Yes, we saw it," Frank said. "Thanks again."

Terry continued driving down the road. Joe

19

looked back at the man and said, "I never trust anyone who wears sunglasses in the dark."

Soon Terry brought the Jeep to the Coalville gas station, which was on the highway just outside of town. A man in a grease-stained jumpsuit was locking the door to the building.

"Hey, Billy," Terry called to the man. "Did Mr. Robinson come by here tonight?"

"Yeah, he came by," Billy said as he walked over to the Jeep. "About an hour ago. He was my last customer. We talked a few minutes, and then he drove off."

"Did he seem all right?" Terry asked.

"He seemed same as always," Billy replied.

"Was there anyone with him?" Frank asked.

"Not a soul," Billy said with a shrug.

"Thanks," Terry said. She put the Jeep in gear and steered it back onto the highway. She drove back to the dirt road and this time continued on to the home of Mr. Wilkins, the lawyer.

Terry and the Hardys were invited inside to tell their story to Wilkins. He listened carefully as he puffed on a pipe.

"I was expecting Clay tonight," Wilkins said with a furrowed brow, "but he hasn't shown up. This is most puzzling."

"Mr. Wilkins," Joe said, "would Clay Robinson have any reason to skip town suddenly?"

"On the contrary," Wilkins said, "things couldn't be going better for Clay. He finally got his development project approved, and he stands to make a sizable amount of money from it."

"Do you know of anyone who might have reason to harm Mr. Robinson?" Frank asked.

The lawyer puffed thoughtfully on his pipe before answering. "A lot of people are opposed to his development project, especially that fella Max Jagowitz. But these are peace-loving people in these parts. I can't imagine any of the locals resorting to violence. All the same, we'd better give a call over to the police station."

"You don't need to bother," Terry said as she stood up. "We'll just drive over there and give a full report."

Fifteen minutes later Terry and the Hardys were in the Coalville Police Station, a small building next to the city hall. The station was nothing more than an office with a few desks and a single jail cell. They told all the details to Sergeant Bunt, a husky young man with a crew cut.

Sergeant Bunt tapped a pencil on his desk. "No, I can't imagine what might have happened to Mr. Robinson," he said. "I've gotten plenty of calls about that orange light, though. Did you all catch a look at that thing?"

"It was amazing," Terry said.

Frank wanted to stay on track. "It seems Robinson disappeared some time between nine-ten and ten-twenty."

21

Sergeant Bunt wrote this down.

"Terry, what are the names of those two bikers?" Joe asked.

"Bev Kominski and Myra Hart," Terry said.

"Oh yes, those the two women I've seen riding all over the place on their bikes?" Bunt said. "They rent the red house at the end of Route Forty-seven."

"Have you had any trouble with them?" Joe asked. "Mr. Robinson fired them a couple of weeks ago, and he said they're really angry about it."

"I've had no trouble with them," Bunt said.

"Mr. Robinson never pressed charges against Bev and Myra," Terry told the Hardys. "We're almost positive they stole some things, but we didn't actually catch them in the act. So Robinson just fired them."

"He should have reported it anyway," Bunt said.

"What should we do about Mr. Robinson?" Joe asked.

"We don't consider a person officially missing until he's gone for forty-eight hours," Bunt said. "But, well, why wait? They're holding the presses down at the local paper so they can write an article about that thing in the sky. I'll tell them to put in something about Robinson's disappearance, too. That way if anyone saw anything,

22

he can call it in. In the meantime I'll do some driving around to look for Robinson."

Bunt leaned back in his chair. "It's funny. Days go by in Moondance Pass with nothing much happening. Then all of a sudden we have a strange night like this. It's almost like that thing in the sky and Robinson's disappearance are related. But, nah, I don't see how that's possible."

Terry and the Hardys left the police station and drove around Moondance Pass for another two hours. With the exception of a deer darting across a road, they saw no one. "I don't think there's anything else we can do tonight," Frank said, yawning. "Let's head back to Silver Crest."

"I guess we'd better," Terry said. "I've got a rafting expedition first thing tomorrow morning. Why don't you guys come along?"

"Rafting—yes!" Joe said enthusiastically.

"Absolutely," Frank added. "We've done all we can for the moment about finding Robinson. We might as well have some fun."

Back at Silver Crest, Terry went to her dorm room at the HQ, and the Hardys walked to the small cabin they were renting.

The cabin was a simple room with two beds, a small kitchenette, and a bathroom, but the place was comfortable and clean.

Frank and Joe washed up quickly and were in

their beds in minutes. Frank drifted off to sleep immediately, but Joe's thoughts kept him wide awake.

"Frank," Joe said after a few minutes, "what do you think the chances are that that was an alien spacecraft we saw tonight?"

"Slim," Frank mumbled. "Joe?" he added.

"What?"

"What do you think the chances are that I'll be getting a good night's sleep? We've got an early morning date with a river tomorrow."

"Party pooper," Joe said, but Frank was already asleep.

Terry, Frank, Joe, and the honeymooners from New York City were rushing through a run of white water in a large inflatable raft early Thursday morning. Two other rafts from Silver Crest were cruising through the waters of the Yukandaya River a short distance ahead. As the guide of her raft, Terry sat in the back, calling out instructions to the passengers.

"Right back!" Terry called.

Those on the right side of the raft paddled energetically while those on the left waited. Depending on the water and the position of the raft, Terry gave various orders to keep the raft on course.

"Everyone back!" Terry called.

Everyone paddled as the raft bounced in the air. Frank winced when a sheet of water flew up and drenched him. At this hour of the morning, eight o'clock, the water was icy.

"Is this great or what?" Joe called as the raft shot through the churning water.

"Fantastic!" Frank called back. "But cold!"

Soon the raft slowed in a calmer section of the river. Terry was able to steer the raft by herself for a while, giving the passengers a chance to relax. "This is so beautiful," the stockbroker's wife observed.

Frank admired the passing scenery. The river was flanked by steep slopes covered with spruce and pine trees. Early morning sunlight glinted on the water. The water was so clear that Frank could see the pebbles on the bottom.

Frank's pleasant thoughts were disturbed by thoughts about Clay Robinson's disappearance. As soon as they had woken up, Frank had called the police station. There had still been no word on Robinson. Before the rafting expedition, Terry had told most of the staff about the Robinson incident, and they had made arrangements how to run Silver Crest without the owner present.

"You might call this the calm before the storm," Terry said as she paddled. "We're coming up on Tombstone Trail."

"What's that?" the stockbroker asked.

"It's the roughest run on the river," Terry said. "It's called Tombstone Trail because some of the rocks are shaped like tombstones."

"That's a relief," Joe said. "I thought it might be because people have died crossing it."

"Not on my expeditions," Terry replied. "But I want you all to make sure you're securely tucked into the boat."

Frank could hear the water roaring again in the distance. Soon the raft was moving more swiftly, and the water churned against big rocks, creating a white foam. Frank tucked his left foot deep into a crevice where the side of the raft met the bottom. He made sure his body was well balanced.

"Here we go!" Terry called out. "Everyone paddle forward!"

Everyone began paddling. The raft blasted forward into what looked like a boiling cauldron. The roar of the river became deafening, and the raft bumped up and down on the rapids as if it were a roller-coaster car. The force of the water threw the raft sideways.

"Left paddle forward!" Terry yelled. Frank lifted his oar from the water as Terry and the left-side passengers paddled.

Then the raft was thrown the other way and it crashed into a boulder right beside Frank. Flying up with the raft, Frank kept his foot securely tucked in.

"Right paddle forward!" Terry yelled, and Frank dug his oar into the rough water.

As the raft shot ahead, Frank found that it was harder to stay balanced now. Perhaps the raft had been damaged by the last boulder, he thought. Before he could say anything to Terry, the raft hit an even wilder stretch of water and vaulted into the air.

Frank slid off the raft and felt the cold water slap him in the face.

He plunged underwater, holding his breath. Then his life jacket jerked him back to the surface. He was on his back, flying through the water so fast that it was as if he had been shot from a cannon.

Frank's senses were assaulted by so many things he could barely separate them—people yelling, the roar of the rapids, the freezing water, the rocks scraping his arms and legs. A boulder flew by, and instinctively Frank grabbed on to it.

The water pounded against Frank's face as he turned to see the raft about thirty yards behind him. Everyone was paddling furiously, and Terry was yelling something Frank couldn't understand. If he could hang on for just a few more moments, he thought, the raft would rescue him.

Then without warning Frank was ripped from the boulder and sent hurtling downriver. Through the foamy spray, Frank glimpsed about a dozen tall rocks jutting up through the water. They were scattered across the width of the river, most of them shaped like tombstones.

Whether he liked it or not, Frank was about to plow into the rocks of Tombstone Trail with terrifying force.

4 An Alien Debate

Frank's heart was pounding as hard as the water. He knew there was no way he could ride past those rocks without serious injury.

His mind raced through his options. He could roll up into a ball to lessen the damage, or he could attempt to grab on to one of the first tombstone-shaped rocks. He chose the second idea.

Scanning the river, Frank picked out a rock. With the water thundering furiously around him, Frank focused all his concentration on that particular rock. He knew he would have only one chance to grab it, and if he missed, he would crash into the rocks that lay just beyond.

A wild cyclone of water suddenly spun Frank

sideways. He whipped his head around to find the rock he wanted. Lifting himself out of the water, he made a desperate lunge.

He threw both arms around the rock. With astonishing power the water wrestled with Frank, trying to tear him away. Frank was not letting go of that precious rock for anything.

"We're coming!" Frank could hear Terry's voice above the roar of the water.

As Frank battled with the water, the raft approached. All of the passengers were paddling backward to keep the raft in place while Terry reached over and grabbed Frank's life jacket. Terry was strong, and soon Frank felt himself being hauled over the side of the raft.

He lay on the bottom of the raft, totally exhausted, but he was still in one piece.

"Everyone paddle forward!" Terry yelled. She paddled left, then right, keeping her eyes on the treacherous rocks of Tombstone Trail. The raft crashed against the rocks and bounced on the swells, but with Terry's expert guidance, it kept on shooting forward.

"The raft got punctured on that rock and that's why you fell out!" Joe called to Frank. "It could have happened to anyone."

Frank nodded, too tired to speak.

As soon as the raft passed safely through Tombstone Trail, Terry guided it to the bank, and everyone hauled it out of the water. Because the raft had lost some air, it was not safe to continue the journey. Soaked to the bone, Terry and the others made their way up a steep bank, then began walking along a narrow dirt trail.

"Are you sure you're okay?" the stockbroker asked Frank as his wife looked on with concern.

"I think so," Frank said. The fact was, he had been extremely lucky. Aside from a few scrapes and cuts, he was fine.

"Does that happen to these rafts very often?" Joe asked Terry.

Terry shook her head. "I've never seen it happen. We check the rafts before each trip and we check them carefully every few days. But when you're up against nature, you can't count on anything."

After a half mile, the group made it to a spot where the two other rafting groups were waiting beside a van. All the rafts were placed on a flatbed attachment that the van drove back to Silver Crest.

There was no sign of Robinson back at the resort. After the Hardys changed into dry clothing, Frank went with Terry to get his minor wounds treated. Joe hit the mess hall for a late breakfast.

The mess hall was a sectioned-off area on the main floor of the HQ. Under the thick wooden beams of the ceiling were several tables and a cafeteria-style counter.

Joe dug into a stack of pancakes, which he had drenched with maple syrup. It was ten o'clock now, and the mess hall was empty. Joe read through a section of the newspaper that covered the Moondance Pass area.

Soon Frank approached the table, a plate of bacon and eggs in his hand.

"I see you're having some pancakes with your syrup," Frank joked as he sat down.

"Mmm," Joe said with a full mouth. Breakfast was too serious to joke about, he decided.

Before long, Terry made it over to the table, carrying a bowl of cereal topped with banana slices. "I just called the police again," she reported. "They say there's still no news on Mr. Robinson. I guess Silver Crest can get by a few days without him, but I'm awfully worried."

"Me, too," Joe said.

"Me three," Frank added.

Terry looked at Frank, then Joe, with a thoughtful expression. "I know something about you guys that I'm not supposed to know," she said.

Frank took a forkful of eggs. "What's that?" he asked.

"That you're detectives," Terry said. "Or at least that you do some detective work now and then. Word gets around school."

Frank and Joe were, in fact, detectives, but they tried to keep it quiet.

32

"Maybe it's true," Joe said, giving Terry a playful glance, "maybe it's not."

"Well, if it is true," Terry said, "what would you guys say to looking into Mr. Robinson's disappearance? Between you, me, and the lamppost, I don't have a lot of faith in the local police. And this is starting to look like a big problem. Clay Robinson could be dead, or he could be in the hands of somebody really dangerous. Or maybe he's running away from someone who's after him."

Joe had been thinking the same thing. Maybe he and Frank should start digging around to see what they could uncover. True, it would cut into their vacation, but the brothers were drawn to mysteries the way a moth is drawn to flame. Besides, a man's life might be at stake.

Joe looked at his brother, and Frank gave a nod. "Okay, we're on the case," Joe told Terry.

"Thank you!" Terry cried.

"Might as well start right now," Frank said. "Does the paper say anything about Robinson?" he asked Joe. "Sergeant Bunt said he would put something in there."

"Yes, there's a short article on Robinson's disappearance," Joe said. "Basically, it just reports the information we gave Bunt. Most of the paper is devoted to that mysterious thing in the sky."

"What do they say about it?" Frank asked.

"A reporter interviewed Alastair Sykes last night," Joe said. "He checked with all the nearby air-traffic centers, and they all claimed there was no commercial aircraft flying in the area at the moment the orange thing appeared. He also checked with several meteorologists, and none of them could identify the description he gave them as being any natural phenomenon they were familiar with."

"Weird," Terry remarked.

Joe finished his last bite of pancake. "There's another interesting detail. Someone at the paper told Sykes about Robinson's disappearance—the abandoned car, the whole thing. Sykes claims Robinson's vanishing has all the earmarks of an alien abduction."

Terry rolled her eyes. "Not surprising. Sykes has aliens on the brain."

Frank thought a moment. "Okay, the first thing for us to consider is who would have a motive for either harming, kidnapping, or killing Clay Robinson."

"We know that a lot of people in town are angry about his development project," Joe said. "Especially that guy Max Jagowitz. And we know Bev and Myra hold a grudge against Robinson because he fired them."

Frank put down his fork. "We know Robinson disappeared somewhere between the time he left the gas station, which was around nine-ten, and when we found his Jeep, which was at ten-twenty."

"We saw Bev and Myra on the road shortly before then," Joe added. "They could have gotten to him. And we saw Jagowitz get into his car not too long after Robinson dropped us off. He could also have gotten to him in that time frame."

"And we saw Alastair Sykes get into his car right after Jagowitz left," Frank pointed out. "Which means he could fit into the time frame as well."

"Why are you concerned about Sykes?" Terry asked.

"Two highly unusual things happened last night," Frank stated. "The orange glow and Robinson's disappearance. Sergeant Bunt thought they might be related, and he may be right. Now, I don't believe the events are related in the way Sykes claims. But I believe he might want us to think they are."

"What are you getting at?" Joe asked.

"It seems important to Sykes that people take his work seriously," Frank said. "That's why he was getting those forms filled out last night. Let's say that after he left the downtown area, he passed Robinson on that deserted road. And let's say he realized if he could make Robinson disappear for a while, it would look as if Robinson had been abducted by aliens. That would mean the orange glow could possibly be an alien space-

35

craft. If all of these things were true, then people might take him more seriously."

Joe grinned. "That sounds like something I might come up with."

"I admit it's a bit far-fetched," Frank said, "but I'd like to check it out anyway."

They sat in silence for a few minutes. Finally Terry said, "You know, it makes you wonder. I've been hearing about this alien stuff for years, and that light was really otherworldly. I seriously doubt Mr. Robinson was abducted by aliens last night, but could that have been an alien spacecraft we saw?"

"Yes," Joe said.

"No," Frank countered.

"Look," Joe said, "I used to think all this alien stuff was a bunch of nonsense, too. But now I'm not so sure. Recently scientists found a rock that had fallen from Mars several thousand years ago. And they found fossils of bacteria in that rock. Bacteria are a life-form!"

"Some scientists say they're bacteria," Frank pointed out. "Others disagree."

"Maybe it is or maybe it isn't," Joe said, "but it really opened my mind to the possibility that there is alien life out there somewhere. And then what about all the UFO sightings? There have been hundreds of unexplained sightings. What we saw last night was technically a sighting, you know."

"That's true," Terry said. "And some of these sightings have been made by very reliable sources. In World War Two, fighter pilots saw mysterious fiery glows outside their planes. And an astronaut saw something like it on one of the first manned space flights."

"There are explanations for these things," Frank said.

"But look—" Joe started.

"The fact is," Frank continued, "there is no real evidence that we have ever been visited by aliens. If there was an authentic photograph or a piece of material from one of these ships, it would be a different story. But there's nothing."

"There's no hard evidence that we *know* about," Joe argued. "But a lot of people think the government has the evidence and is keeping it a secret."

"Okay," Frank said, breaking a piece of bacon in half. "For now why don't we agree to disagree on this?"

Joe let out a long breath. Frank refused to believe in *anything* unless the evidence was set down right in front of him.

"All right," Joe said, "let's get to work. First, why don't we pay a visit to Alastair Sykes?"

"I can give you directions to his house," Terry said. "I'd take you there myself, but I've got to take another group on the river in about an hour. I am free this afternoon. How about I take you up to Moondance Peak? The view from there is awesome."

After finishing breakfast, the Hardys borrowed Robinson's Jeep and set off down the highway. Since they had flown into Colorado, Frank and Joe were without their trusty van, but the Jeep was especially good for maneuvering in the rugged terrain.

"Look at that," Joe said, leaning out the passenger window. By daylight the mountains were magnificent. They stretched in every direction, some of them sloping gently, and others rising into high, jagged peaks. Covered with evergreen trees, moss, and dirt, every mountain was distinctive and looked like a colorful artistic creation.

Following Terry's directions, Frank soon came to a house halfway up a small mountain. It was a three-story structure with a sky blue wooden exterior.

Frank parked the Jeep, and the Hardys approached the front door. There was an intercom box, which seemed odd for such an old home. Frank pushed the buzzer. "Hello," an electronically amplified voice said.

Frank assumed the voice belonged to Sykes. "Hi, this is Frank and Joe Hardy," Frank told the box. "We filled out forms for you last night."

The front door buzzed, opening the door, and the Hardys entered the house. They stood in a hallway with family photographs lining one wall.

Adjoining the hall was a living room, decorated with antique furniture. The place was nice but a bit dusty.

At first no one seemed to be around, but then Joe noticed someone—or something—in the living room. Joe felt his jaw drop open. "Whoa," he whispered.

Sitting on a sofa was some sort of creature. Its body vaguely resembled that of a human, except its flesh was gray and hairless. The head was shaped like an upside-down pear. The only features on the face were two large black, unblinking eyes.

5 Visitors

Joe took a few steps into the living room, focusing on the creature. Then he stopped. He thought he saw the creature's head move, but then realized it might have been shifting light slanting in through a window.

"Frank, what in the world is this?" Joe whispered.

Frank stepped into the living room and approached the creature slowly. He reached out and touched the creature's arm. He turned to Joe. "I hate to disappoint you, but it's not real. It's made of rubber."

"It could have fooled me," Joe said.

There was a chuckle, and both Hardys turned to see Alastair Sykes watching them from the hallway. "I see you met my buddy Felix," he said. "He was used in a Hollywood movie and I bought him a few years back at an auction. He's designed to resemble the type of alien that many people have claimed to have seen. I live alone in this big house, and I guess he keeps me company. Now, what can I do for you fellows?"

Sykes was dressed casually in khakis and a pullover sweater. He seemed pleased the Hardys were there.

Joe stuck his hands in his pockets, hoping he'd appear to be just a curious teenager. He didn't want Sykes to know he and Frank were investigating Robinson's disappearance.

"We wanted to hear a little more about your work," Joe said.

Sykes adjusted his glasses. "I'm pretty busy today, but I guess I can find some time. Follow me."

Sykes led the Hardys along the hallway toward the back of the house to a large room that had no resemblance to the rest of the house. It was spotlessly clean and was fitted out with all sorts of high-tech equipment. Joe noticed several computers and what appeared to be very sophisticated audio decks. Hung on one wall was a vast chart of the Milky Way.

"I had this room added on a few years back," Sykes said proudly. "Welcome to my laboratory."

Frank realized things were moving in the

room. Waves wriggled by on a computer screen, digital numbers shifted on several decks, and a printer was spewing out an unending sheet of paper that folded itself on the floor. A faint sound of static buzzed throughout the room.

"Laboratory for what?" Frank asked.

Sykes fixed his magnified eyes on Frank. "For communicating with extraterrestrials. Though I prefer to call them Visitors. It sounds friendlier. Of course, I don't know yet if they're friendly or not, but I like to give everyone the benefit of the doubt."

"I thought you said you communicated with them," Frank commented.

"No, I am *attempting* to communicate with them," Sykes said. "I'm a radio astronomer, you see. I used to work in the SETI program."

"I've read about SETI," Joe said, bending to glance at a piece of equipment. "It stands for Search for Extraterrestrial Intelligence, right?"

"Correct," Sykes said. "SETI programs have been around since the sixties. Most of them are based in various universities and observatories around the world. Here, please take a look."

Sykes indicated a large window. Both Hardys looked outside. A little way up the mountain was a white device that resembled a television satellite dish, but larger.

"SETI programs utilize radio astronomy,"

Sykes said, "and what you're looking at is a radio telescope. You see, the largest optical telescopes don't show enough for us to determine if there are alien civilizations in the far reaches of the universe. So to find these civilizations, we don't look. We listen."

"How will these telescopes find those civilizations?" Frank asked.

"If the civilizations are technologically advanced," Sykes said, "chances are they're sending out some kind of radio waves, just as we do when we broadcast television and radio programs. And, you see, radio telescopes are capable of receiving these signals from great distances. There's a radio telescope in Puerto Rico that can receive waves from a distance of twenty-four-thousand light-years. That's almost a hundred and fifty *billion* miles!"

"How will you know if you've received an alien signal?" Joe asked.

Sykes stole a look at the spewing paper, then turned back to the Hardys. "Good question. You see, there're all kinds of random noises in space. In fact, that's what this static sound is that you're hearing. But if we hear a sound with a repeating pattern, we can be fairly certain it's a wave that has been created by some form of civilization."

Joe thought this was fascinating. The idea of actually making contact with alien beings filled him with wonder. "But SETI programs have never picked up anything from aliens," he said. "Have they?"

Sykes shook his head. "Alas, not yet."

Of course not, Frank thought. Unlike Joe, he felt there was little chance anyone would be communicating with ETs anytime soon. But he was interested in Sykes and his research because the man might somehow be connected to Robinson's disappearance.

"Why did you leave the SETI program?" Frank asked.

Sykes sat in a swivel chair. "I was let go a few years back when the government pulled the plug on most of SETI's funding. But I was planning to quit anyway."

"Why?" Frank said.

"There's overwhelming evidence that 'Visitors' have been exploring earth for centuries," Sykes said. "Yet the governments of the world, especially ours, consistently deny this evidence. They even go to great lengths to cover it up."

"Why would the government do that?" Joe asked.

"Because," Sykes said, fixing his magnified eyes on Joe, "these Visitors would have very sophisticated technology, which the government would love to get its hands on for military purposes. For this reason I think ETs avoid communicating with SETI because they know the government would immediately rush in and take over the investigation."

"So you feel," Frank said, "the ETs would be more likely to communicate with an independent scientist like yourself. Someone not connected to any large organization?"

"Exactly," Sykes said excitedly.

"Well, your equipment is certainly nice," Frank said, "but isn't it too small for this kind of research?"

"For picking up signals from the far reaches of space, yes," Sykes said. "But not for making contact with Visitors already in our neighborhood, so to speak. The telescope in my backyard works fine for that. As long as they're somewhere below the exosphere, they can find me and send a signal. And there's evidence they're in the neighborhood frequently."

"How will they know they can trust *you?*" Frank asked. He wasn't sure if he should burst out laughing or pretend to believe what Sykes was saying.

"Because," Sykes said, "unlike the SETI program, I'm not just listening—I'm talking. You see, I've devised a language for communicating with these Visitors."

Sykes paused to fix his gaze on Frank and Joe before he continued. "If they've come this far, obviously their technology and intelligence will be sophisticated enough to decipher my language. When I suspect they might be listening, I send out messages."

Frank looked around the lab. "Who pays for all this stuff?"

Sykes showed a modest smile. "A very generous and brilliant person by the name of Alastair Sykes. I pay for it myself. My great-grandfather made a large fortune during the old Colorado mining days. Both my parents have passed on, and since I was an only child their money has come to me. This money is what I live on, and it's allowed me to buy all these expensive toys. But unfortunately . . ." Sykes hesitated.

"Unfortunately what?" Joe asked.

"The well is running dry," Sykes said, removing his glasses to clean them. "In other words, I'm almost out of money. I've applied to several scientific foundations for funding, but it's very difficult to get them to take my work seriously. That's part of the reason I needed those forms filled out last night. I need to convince these organizations that Visitors are with us. Now."

"According to you," Frank pointed out.

Sykes rose to his feet. "No, not just me. According to hundreds of other people, too. Are you familiar with the abduction phenomenon?"

"I am," Joe said. "A lot of people claim aliens have abducted them for brief periods of time and taken them aboard their spacecraft. But for some reason these people have only very dim memories of their experiences."

"The phenomenon is called missing time," Sykes said, putting his glasses back on. "The abductees seem to black out from the moment the Visitors take them to the moment they are returned. But under hypnosis with licensed psychotherapists, most of these people are able to recall their experiences very clearly."

"Don't these people claim that the aliens examined them in some way?" Frank asked.

"Correct," Sykes answered. "And most of their memories are very similar, meaning it's unlikely they're making up their stories. And, let me point out, these people are not lunatics. They are sane, intelligent, and thoroughly believable."

Sykes indicated a shelf where audiocassettes were stored, each with a label. "You see these?" he asked. "These are tapes of some of those hypnosis sessions. I don't have time to play them for you right now, but some other time I will and then you will be convinced these alien encounters are real."

Frank listened to the static for a moment, then wondered what else he should find out from Sykes. "We know you're busy," Frank said, "but before we go, let me ask you this. Why do you suppose the aliens chose Clay Robinson to abduct?"

Sykes opened his arms in a gesture of puzzlement. "Maybe because he was driving along a deserted road and they knew they could take him without any witnesses. That seems to be common. Or maybe they were attracted to his red hair. Or maybe because he stole some moonstones twenty years ago. We're dealing with alien minds. At this point it's impossible to know what they're thinking."

Frank wrinkled his brow. "What was that about moonstones?" he said.

"Oh, I didn't really mean anything by that," Sykes said with a dismissive wave. "But I don't mind saying I'm extremely disappointed they took Robinson. The man is not worthy of such an encounter. As long as the Visitors were whistling through Moondance Pass, they should have taken me!"

"So you would like to be abducted?" Joe asked.

Behind the glasses, Alastair Sykes's eyes seemed to twinkle. "Would I like to meet an intelligent life-form from another planet? That would be the greatest scientific adventure imaginable!"

Frank was beginning to feel he had heard enough. He headed for the door. "Okay, Mr. Sykes, we really appreciate—"

Something in the room began beeping loudly, and now there was a buzzing noise on top of the static. Frank noticed letters lit up on one of the decks. A message read, "Possible Signal of ET Origin."

Joe sprang up. "What's happening?"

"Shh!" Sykes said as he raced to study the computer screen. He reached out to examine the paper that spilled from the printer.

"Yes!" Sykes exclaimed as he began pushing buttons on several decks. "I'm getting distinctly nonrandom signals from some point in the upper ionosphere!"

"What does that mean?" Frank asked. In spite of his doubts, Frank felt his heartbeat speed up with anticipation.

Sykes sat down and put on a headset. "That means this could be it!" he cried. "My first communication with the Visitors!"

6 The Black Elk

Frank and Joe watched as Sykes listened to his headset. The beeping, buzzing, and printing continued.

Joe's eyes were aglow. At this very moment, he thought, Alastair Sykes might be receiving a communication from an intelligent being from another planet. Maybe the Visitors who had caused the orange UFO were the ones sending the message.

Then Sykes slowly took off the headset. He sat there a moment, as if absorbing the shock of bad news.

"What happened?" Joe asked.

Sykes sighed. "False alarm. I was picking up

salsa music from a very powerful radio station in Mexico."

Frank tried to conceal a smile as Sykes began pushing buttons. Soon the beeping and buzzing stopped, and the screen no longer carried the Possible Signal message.

"You had me going for a second," Joe said.

"Sorry about that," Sykes replied. "So far it's only been false alarms. But I guarantee you, one day the Visitors and I are going to communicate. And after what happened last night, I think that day may be closer than you think."

"That would be truly amazing," Joe told Sykes.

Sykes pulled a booklet from a shelf and handed it to Joe. "Here's a pamphlet I've created. It tells you all about my work. Take it, please."

"Thanks," Joe said. The pamphlet was titled *The Independent Quest to Find Alien Visitors.*

"I'll have to let you out," Sykes said, moving to the door. "I've got a sophisticated security system throughout the house. The place was burglarized once, and I don't want it to happen again."

As the Hardys drove away from the house, Joe said, "You think he's crazy, don't you?"

"No, I think he's a smart guy barking up the wrong tree," Frank said as he steered the Jeep. "I'm glad we came here, though. We learned two things that support my theory about Sykes being the one who made Robinson disappear."

"Let me guess," Joe said. "Reason one: Sykes doesn't seem to like Robinson. And what was that comment about Robinson having stolen some moonstones?"

"I don't know," Frank said. "He sort of took the comment back. That was very strange."

"Reason two," Joe continued. "Sykes desperately needs people to believe ETs are around so he can get some funding money."

"Right," Frank agreed.

Although Joe didn't say it out loud, another possibility had crept into his mind. Maybe Clay Robinson *had* really been abducted by aliens. It seemed like an awfully big coincidence that Robinson had disappeared on the same night the orange UFO appeared.

Joe wondered if there was anyone connected to the U.S. government whom they could contact—someone who might have some real answers about whether or not aliens had ever visited the earth.

Frank's voice interrupted Joe's thoughts. "I say we keep a close eye on Sykes," he said. "But for now let's move on to some more earthly suspects."

It was around one o'clock now, and the day was turning warm. Out the window, Joe saw a grassy meadow filled with yellow and scarlet wildflowers. The scene was so pretty, Joe thought, that it could be on a postcard. "So, who are these earthly suspects we're going to talk to?" he asked Frank.

"Sergeant Bunt said Bev and Myra live in the red house at the end of Route Forty-seven," Frank said. "We're on Route Forty-seven now. I thought we could stop by their place. Who knows? They might even be holding Robinson hostage."

Soon the Jeep came to an area of modest homes, and Frank parked in front of one that was painted bright red. Joe knocked at the door, but there was no answer. Joe walked to the side of the house and noticed curtains blowing through an open window.

"Should we have a look inside?" Frank asked, coming up behind Joe.

Frank glanced around to make sure no one was watching. "Keep a lookout for me," he said, and put his hands on the windowsill to hoist himself up and into the house.

Frank stood in a living room filled with worn-out furniture. The place smelled musty, and it was a mess—littered with pizza boxes, soda cans, magazines, and all sorts of biking gear.

Frank checked the bathroom and two bedrooms, looking for any sign that Clay Robinson might have been there. He hoped there would be a clue to indicate that Bev and Myra had done something with him. Frank looked through everything, including the piles of dirty clothes in

53

the bedrooms. Aside from the mess, he found nothing even remotely suspicious. After checking to make sure there was no basement, Frank climbed back out the window.

"Did you find anything?" Joe asked.

"If being a bad housekeeper is a crime," Frank said, "we could make a citizen's arrest. But other than a lot of clothes lying around, I found nothing at all."

Frank took off for the Jeep. "But we should try to talk with Bev and Myra later. For now let's move on to our next suspect—Mr. Max Jagowitz."

The Hardys drove into downtown Coalville and, after parking, stepped through the screen-door entrance of the Black Elk. The store was one big room with wide wood plank floors. All around, shelves and racks were stocked with foods, essential supplies, and recreational gear. A gigantic elk's head with antlers was mounted on one wall.

The store was empty except for Jagowitz, who sat in a rocking chair. He looked comfortable in his overalls and baseball cap as he creaked slowly back and forth in the chair.

"That's quite an elk," Frank remarked in his friendliest manner.

"Thank you," Jagowitz said with a modest nod. "Shot it myself. One of the largest antler racks on record. That was one smart animal, let me tell you. Tracked it for half a day before I brought it down. Are you boys hunters?"

They were, Joe thought, but not in the way Jagowitz meant. "No, not us," Joe said with a chuckle.

"Too bad," Jagowitz said. He gestured to a section of the store with hunting and fishing equipment. "I've got guns, shells, knives—everything a hunter needs."

The Hardys ambled over to look at the equipment, not because they needed anything but because they didn't want Jagowitz to suspect the real purpose of their visit. Soon Frank turned to Jagowitz. "So, you've lived in Moondance Pass a long time?" he said.

"That's right," Jagowitz said. "My whole life."

As Joe looked at the supplies, Frank chatted with Jagowitz. His goal was to get Jagowitz talking to see if anything useful came out of the old man's mouth. "I take it Coalville was once a big mining town," Frank said.

Jagowitz rocked a moment, then spoke. "First the Indians came to these parts, living off the elk. Then the trappers came, searching out the beavers. Then the prospectors came, hauling all their possessions on a burro's back. They found silver to the west and gold to the north, but here they found coal. Lots of it. That's about when my family first came here—1889."

"Where did your people come from?" Frank asked.

"My great-granddad came here from Yugoslavia," Jagowitz said with pride. "At least at that time they called it Yugoslavia. He worked the mines. So did my granddad, my dad, and myself for a spell. And let me tell you, that was some tough work—digging out the tunnels and hauling carts loaded with coal. All of it in the pitch-dark, mind you. Knowing if you weren't careful with your lamp, the coal gases might ignite and blow you to bits."

"When did the mines close down?" Frank asked.

"Early 1950s," Jagowitz replied. "Everything started running on electricity and oil, and mining the coal wasn't so profitable anymore. A lot of folks left the area then. Not me, though. I wanted to stay on, so I opened the store."

Frank felt Jagowitz was looking at him with just a hint of suspicion in his eyes. Just then Joe sauntered over. "You must like it here," Joe remarked in a tone as friendly as Frank's.

"Can you blame me?" Jagowitz said with a shrug.

"No, sir," Joe replied. "It's some of the most gorgeous country I've ever seen."

Frank decided it was time to probe Max Jagowitz a little deeper. "It's so peaceful here," he said. "It almost seems a shame Clay Robinson is building that big hotel and condominium complex."

Jagowitz stopped rocking. When he spoke anger thickened his gravelly voice. *"Almost* a shame? It's the biggest shame I ever heard of. Look, I'm not against sharing this beautiful place with folks who want to enjoy it. Fine with me if we've got some resort villages, and, of course, people are certainly free to build homes out here. But this big, glitzy affair Robinson's building, the Golden Dream . . . well, that's different."

Jagowitz paused and stared into space for a moment. "I can see it now. People clogging the roads in their fancy cars. Then they'll build stores and nightclubs. Eventually they'll put up an airport so we can have planes zooming overhead, ruining our sleep. I say this was meant to be peaceful country, but if Robinson has his way, the only place I'll get any peace is in my grave!"

As Frank and Joe nodded in sympathy, a middle-aged woman entered the store. "Hi there, Max," she said cheerfully. "I just need some paper towels today."

"Anything you want," Jagowitz said, rising from his chair.

The woman picked up a roll of paper towels. As Jagowitz rang up her purchase at the antique cash register, the two began chatting.

Frank didn't want to leave just yet. He felt he had touched a nerve with the talk of the Golden

Dream, and he wanted to pursue the topic a little further. He saw Joe walk to a pay phone and make a call. "Who were you calling?" Frank asked when Joe returned.

Joe gestured in Jagowitz's direction. "Uh, I think I'll tell you later."

Frank gave Joe a playful punch on the arm. "Hey, you're not supposed to keep secrets from your big brother. Come on, tell me who it was."

"Later," Joe said with a sly smile.

Even though he had eaten a big breakfast, Joe knew he would be getting hungry again soon. He picked up a bag of potato chips from a rack and placed two quarters on the counter near the cash register. He didn't want to interrupt the conversation between Jagowitz and the woman.

Soon the woman left the store, and Jagowitz returned to his rocking chair. Frank picked up where he had left off. "I'm surprised no one has tried to do any big developing before this," Frank told Jagowitz.

"Oh, they've tried," Jagowitz said. "But there's a council that oversees all the affairs of the Moondance Pass area. I'm a member myself. And we've got very strict ordinances against large-scale development around here."

"How did the Golden Dream get around the ordinances?" Joe asked.

Jagowitz creaked back and forth in the chair.

58

"Robinson asked the council to make an exception for his project. He said his complex would bring a lot of jobs to the area and he would do everything very tastefully. Promised he wouldn't ruin Moondance Pass but make it better. He made a good pitch and got some of the council members eating out of his hand. The council voted to lift the ordinance just for Robinson by a vote of five to four."

"You must have been unhappy," Frank said.

Jagowitz gave a hoarse chuckle. "I hollered till the hills started shaking. But there wasn't much else I could do, was there?"

Jagowitz glanced at the door as a man wearing a fisherman's vest entered the store. Frank had one more question he needed to ask before leaving. "Do you have any idea what might have happened to Robinson last night?" he said.

Jagowitz narrowed his eyes. "No, I don't. I'm not the type to wish harm to anyone, but maybe it's best if he stays where he is."

"Where he is? What—" Frank began, but he was interrupted by the fisherman.

"Hey, Max," the fisherman called out, "I need a good knife for gutting fish."

Jagowitz rose from his chair. "Well, I got the best knife collection in the Rockies. Come on, let's pick one out for you."

Frank watched Jagowitz move to the knife

counter. Frank signaled to Joe, and they passed through the entrance. When they were outside, Joe said, "So, what do you think?"

Just then the screen door flew open and Jagowitz seized Joe roughly by the wrist. There was a fierce look in the old man's eyes.

"Young fella," Jagowitz growled like a grizzly bear, "I see now why you and your brother came into my store. And I don't like it one bit!"

7 Terror at Ten Thousand Feet

Jagowitz kept Joe's wrist in his clawlike grip. "You think I don't know what you're up to, don't you?" he said angrily.

"What are you talking about?" Joe asked in confusion.

"I see what you've got in your hand," Jagowitz said. "And who knows what you've got in your pockets."

When Joe saw that Jagowitz was referring to the bag of potato chips he was still holding, he realized Jagowitz thought he had stolen the chips.

"I paid for these," Joe said. "While you were talking to that woman, I left two quarters on the counter."

"He's telling the truth," Frank said evenly. "My brother has never stolen anything in his life."

Jagowitz's glare melted. He released Joe's wrist. "Okay. I'll take your word for it. I'm just jumpy these days, knowing this whole area is about to change. I'm thinking there's going to be all kinds of crime once that Golden Dream monstrosity opens. Come back to my store anytime, boys."

Jagowitz entered the store, and the Hardys walked along the street in silence for a few minutes.

"What a temper," Joe said. "And he's pretty strong for someone who's nearly eighty years old."

"Must be the mountain air," Frank said with a chuckle. "As I started to say," he added, "Max Jagowitz feels as though his family founded Coalville. He likes the town the way it is and takes it as a personal insult that Robinson wants to jazz things up. But kidnapping Robinson wouldn't accomplish anything. Robinson would just pick up where he left off as soon as he was released. To do any good, Jagowitz would have to kill Robinson."

Joe caught Frank's eyes. "The way he was talking, I wouldn't be surprised if tomorrow we see a stuffed Robinson hanging on the wall next to the elk."

"Very funny," Frank said with a groan. "But I do wonder what we should do now."

Joe checked his watch. "Right now we'd better get back to Silver Crest. Remember, Terry wants to take us to the top of Moondance Peak this afternoon."

The brothers stopped in front of the post office. "Why don't you two make the excursion without me?" Frank said. "I want to hang around Coalville awhile and see what else I can learn. I'm sure I can hitch a ride back to Silver Crest. I'll meet you there sometime around six."

"Okay," Joe said. "Just don't get yourself abducted by aliens."

"And don't you, either," Frank said with a grin.

Joe felt as if he were sailing over the treetops, watching as the base of the mountain grew farther and farther away. He and Terry were riding up Moondance Peak in a rickety but still-working ski lift.

"Is this a view or what?" Terry asked.

"The best," Joe said as he took in the expanse below. Clouds drifting over the mountains seemed close enough to touch.

After a twenty-minute ride, the ski chair angled to the ground, then was stopped by an operator sitting in a booth. Joe and Terry hopped out of the chair and began walking along a narrow dirt trail. If this had been ski season they would have skied down the mountain, but today they were walking up.

"These trees are incredible," Joe said, admiring the evergreens that towered on either side of the trail.

"Hey, try this," Terry said, going up to a pine tree and sniffing its bark.

Joe put his nose next to the bark. "Mmm, nice."

As Joe stepped back on the trail, he heard something crunching over gravel and pinecones. A bicycle came barreling at them, almost knocking the pair over. "Hey, watch it!" Terry yelled as the biker flew past.

The cyclist expertly spun the bike around and braked at the same time. A cloud of dust filled the air. The sturdy frame and thick wheels told Joe this was a mountain bike, perfect for rugged terrain.

Joe realized this was one of the women who had swerved in front of Robinson's Jeep the night before. Joe guessed she was in her early twenties. Beneath the biker's helmet, Joe could see short blond hair that framed a scowling face.

"Hi, Bev," Terry said, her voice suddenly tense.

"Well, if it isn't Tattletale Terry," Bev said in a sarcastic tone. "Don't you have something better

64

to do? Like spying on someone who's supposed to be a friend!"

Terry grimaced. "I don't have friends who steal."

"Well, aren't you the goody-goody," Bev said. "Say, how's the rafting business these days?"

A look of anger crossed Terry's face. "Why do you ask?"

"No reason," Bev answered as she spun her bike around. She began pedaling down the trail, spraying more dust in the air.

"So that was Bev of Bev and Myra fame," Joe said as he brushed dust off his jeans.

"Right," Terry said.

"Why did you get so angry when she asked about the rafting business?" Joe said.

"Here's why," Terry said. "After you guys left this morning, I talked to the other rafting guides about our accident on the river. One of the guides told me he thoroughly checked all the rafts last night and found them all to be just fine."

"Uh-huh," Joe said with interest.

"But that same guide," Terry continued, "remembered seeing Bev and Myra riding past the resort shortly after that. Then when Bev asked about the rafting business in that sarcastic tone of hers, it made me think that maybe Bev and Myra went into the storage bin and put a small puncture in one of the rafts. When they were fired, they turned in all their keys, but who knows which ones they might have copied?"

"Makes sense that they'd do that to get back at Robinson for firing them," Joe said.

"You got it," Terry answered.

Joe and Terry continued up the trail. "Tell me more about the theft," Joe said. "What actually happened?"

"Robinson has a small office in the HQ," Terry told him. "He's got a safe in there, which he usually keeps locked. One night he left the office for a few minutes. I was walking down the hall, and I saw Bev and Myra coming out of the office. I didn't think anything of it until later when Robinson mentioned some things were missing from the safe. So I told Robinson what I saw."

"So there wasn't any actual proof that they stole anything?" Joe said.

"No," Terry answered. "I guess that's why Robinson never pressed charges. He never even told me what was stolen. All the same, it seems pretty obvious Bev and Myra were the culprits."

"Interesting," Joe said.

The trail grew steeper, causing Joe to breathe harder as they climbed. Soon he and Terry reached the timberline. Above Joe and Terry, the rest of the mountain had no trees at all.

"Tell me a little about Clay Robinson," Joe said as he and Terry scrambled over dirt and gray rock. "It might help us if we had more background on the guy."

"I know he grew up in Coalville," Terry said. "His father was a janitor or something like that. I get the impression the family didn't have much money. After high school Robinson did some construction work, then he left this area when he was in his twenties."

"Where did he go?" Joe asked.

"He went to New Mexico and got into the land-developing business," Terry said. "I guess he did pretty well, money-wise. Then five years ago he moved back here and bought Silver Crest."

Joe paused to catch his breath. "This altitude is amazing. Do you know anything about his family life?"

Terry paused. "He supports his parents, who live in Florida now. He was married for a while in New Mexico, but he and his wife split up before he came back here. I suppose he knows a lot of people, but he doesn't seem to have many close friends. That's part of the reason I asked you and Frank to get involved in this. I'm not sure there's anybody else concerned about his welfare."

"Except for Stella," Joe said.

"That's true," Terry said with a nod. "He really loves that dog. And the feeling is mutual. I kept Stella in my room last night, and she really seemed to miss him."

Joe and Terry began to climb again. "Do you

know if there's bad feeling between Robinson and his ex-wife?'' Joe asked.

"Sorry, I don't,'' Terry said. "I've spent a lot of time around Mr. Robinson, but he's not the kind of person you get to know well. Sometimes I think he keeps his personal life locked up in that safe.''

After a short distance Terry and Joe were almost at the peak. Shielding his eyes, Joe gazed down at the surrounding mountains. He could actually see clouds floating below him now.

Terry clapped Joe on the shoulder. "Congratulations. You're now twelve thousand feet above sea level. That's two miles high. This is probably the closest you'll ever get to touching the sky with your feet on the ground.''

Joe took a deep breath. "Frank is really missing something,'' he said.

"Hey, do me a favor,'' Terry said. She handed Joe an automatic camera. "I want you to get a picture of me on the peak.''

The uppermost portion of the mountain was extremely steep, but Terry began clambering over the rocks as if she'd been born there. "Careful!'' Joe called as he readied the camera.

"Come on, you're talking to Mountain Woman,'' Terry called back. But she spoke too soon. Several steps later she slipped and tumbled a few yards down the incline, bumping against the jagged rocks. She was able to get up, but Joe saw she was gritting her teeth in pain.

"Hey, Mountain Woman," Joe called as he climbed up toward her, "are you all right?"

"I guess," Terry called back. Joe could see she was holding her left arm. "But my wrist is killing me."

"Can you move your fingers?" Joe asked, still moving toward her.

Terry gave it a try. "Not really," she said.

"It could be broken," Joe said. He took Terry's right arm and helped her down the rocks. "We have to get you to a doctor on the double."

Terry was still in pain when she and Joe reached the ski lift booth. They walked to the window of the booth so they could get the operator to stop the lift for them. A young woman with earphones stood in the booth, listening to a radio.

When the woman turned, a sneer crossed her face. "Well, hello, little Miss Tattletale."

Joe realized this was Myra. She was tall with long, glossy black hair. Joe thought she looked about the same age as Bev.

"Myra," Terry said with surprise. "I didn't see you when we came up. I didn't know you worked here."

"I have to work somewhere," Myra said, giving her long hair a toss. "Remember, you got me fired from my last job. And, oh, I'm on the afternoon shift. I just got here."

"Look, Myra," Terry said, irritated, "I'm sorry if I caused any trouble for you and Bev. I just reported what I saw."

Myra rolled her eyes. "Well, I guess Robinson might have gotten what was coming to him anyway. Wherever he is now."

Joe stepped forward. "Why do you say that? Do you have an idea where he might be?"

Myra turned to Joe. "Are you talking to me? I don't believe I know you."

"My name is Joe Hardy," Joe said firmly. "Do you have any idea where Clay Robinson might be?"

"No clue, buddy," Myra said as she turned away. "Have a nice ride down." With that, Myra pressed a button to stop a ski chair for Joe and Terry.

Joe wanted to interrogate Myra further, but getting Terry to a doctor was more important. He helped Terry into a chair, got in himself, and pulled down the safety bar. The chair moved forward with a lurch.

"How's your wrist doing?" Joe asked.

"It hurts like crazy," Terry said.

As the chair moved down the mountain, Joe noticed a cluster of dark clouds hovering over a nearby mountain. There was a gray haze below the clouds, and Joe realized it was raining there.

After about five minutes, the chair stopped.

Joe looked around. "What happened?"

"I don't know," Terry replied. "I hope it's not any kind of mechanical trouble."

Joe and Terry sat for several minutes, but the chair didn't start to move again. Terry shook her head with disgust. "You know, I'll bet Myra stopped the lift to spite me."

"She does seem to have a lot of spite in her," Joe said. "How long do you think she'll make us stay here?"

"Knowing her," Terry said, "it could be the rest of the day."

The operator's booth was now out of view. Joe realized Myra was probably too far away to hear him if he yelled, especially if she'd put her radio earphones on again.

Joe spotted one of the cable poles that stood several feet in front of the chair. The pole had a ladder that led to the ground.

"I'm climbing down," Joe said. "I'll get Myra to start this thing up again."

"Forget it," Terry said. She grabbed Joe's arm. "If you fall, you could break a leg and then we'll be worse off than we are now."

Joe pondered the situation. He figured there was about a three-story drop from the chair to the ground. "I have another leg, you know." He hoped he sounded brave, but he really felt scared.

"Joe, no!" Terry cried.

Joe knew this wasn't the smartest thing in the world, but he also knew he had a pretty good chance he'd make it to the pole.

He stepped on the seat and grabbed hold of a metal bar above his head. The chair rocked slightly. Joe placed a foot on the safety bar, tested it, then put his other foot on the bar.

The chair rocked a little more. Joe waited for it to stop. Then, keeping one hand on the bar above him, he reached with the other hand for a rung of the ladder. His fingers were a few inches short of their target.

Joe shifted his weight on to one leg, sent the other leg back for balance, and stretched his arm out farther.

Suddenly the chair began to move again.

Terry cried out in horror.

A lightning bolt of fear pulsed through Joe's body as he toppled forward and found himself falling!

8 Thin Air

Joe shot his hand out. He managed to catch hold of a metal bar on the side of the chair. He hung dangling from the chair as it moved down the mountain.

"Hang on!" Terry called. She reached down and grabbed Joe's arm with her good hand.

"Not a chance I'm going to let go," Joe called back.

Joe tried to get his other hand onto the bar, but the angle was awkward, and the chair's motion did not make things easy.

Holding the bar with her injured hand, Terry struggled to haul Joe up with her other hand. "I can't get you!" she called.

Joe kept dangling, but the arm with which he

was holding on was growing tired. He glanced at the grassy ground moving below. He wondered if he should just risk a fall. But even if he did a tuck-and-roll landing, he knew he'd be looking at a few days in the hospital.

"I'm coming up!" Joe called.

With a burst of effort, Joe kicked out his legs and swung his body. He caught the bar with his other hand. Then he pulled himself high enough so Terry was able to grab hold of him under the arms and pull him back into the chair.

Joe and Terry collapsed on the chair, both of them breathing hard.

"I shouldn't have eaten all those pancakes this morning," Joe said.

"I think you just worked them off," Terry said with a laugh. "Now will you promise me you won't get out of the chair until we get to the bottom of the mountain?"

"I'm so tired, I may not get out of the chair when we do reach the bottom of the mountain," Joe said, breathing hard.

Joe and Terry didn't return to Silver Crest until seven. Terry was now wearing a lightweight fiberglass splint on her left wrist. According to the doctor, the wrist was sprained, rather than broken, but it was enough to keep her away from her duties as guide for a few days.

There was still no word on Robinson. By this

time his disappearance was the main topic of discussion among the Silver Crest staff and guests.

Frank had bought sandwiches, potato salad, and soft drinks in town. He, Terry, and Joe sat outside on a blanket and had a picnic dinner.

After Joe and Terry related their close call on Moondance Peak, Frank had a few things to report. "I talked to several people in town," he began. "Apparently there was a real tug-of-war between Jagowitz and Robinson when the council voted on the Golden Dream. Robinson told everybody that Jagowitz was a crazy old codger living in the past. Jagowitz told everyone that Robinson would sell his own mother to make a dime."

"Harsh words," Joe said, chewing a bite of sandwich. "No telling where things could have led."

Stella was lying at Joe's feet, watching every movement of the food with great interest.

"Did you find out anything new about Bev and Myra?" Terry asked as she handed the dog a bite of meat.

"Maybe," Frank said. "I found a guy who's into mountain biking. He said he heard a rumor they'd been arrested for theft in another town a while back."

"If they do have an arrest record," Joe said, "that would make them nervous about getting arrested again. Maybe they were afraid Robinson would change his mind about pressing charges and decided to fix it so he couldn't."

"Possibly," Frank said. "But remember, that was only a rumor about their arrest."

Joe dug into the potato salad. "We have a strong motive for all of our suspects—Jagowitz, Bev, Myra, Sykes. And they were all in the vicinity when Robinson disappeared last night. But we still can't pin the crime on any of them. And, you know, they might all be innocent."

Terry put a hand on Stella. "Where is Clay Robinson?" she said quietly.

Stella let out a low whimper. It might have been a request for food, Joe thought, or it might have been because she missed her owner.

After their picnic everyone put on jackets as the air turned cooler and night descended.

"Phone call for Joe Hardy!" someone called from the HQ.

Joe ran to the HQ while Terry and Frank walked over to play a game of moonlight horseshoes. By the time Joe returned, Terry had already beaten Frank by a wide margin.

"Don't sweat it," Terry told Frank. "I get a lot more practice than you."

"Who was on the phone?" Frank asked.

"That was General Radman," Joe said with a sly smile.

"Really?" Frank said. General Radman was an

Air Force general who was a friend of their father, Fenton Hardy. "How did Radman know you were here, and what did he want?" Frank asked.

"That's who I was calling on the pay phone at the Black Elk," Joe said. "I wanted to see if he could arrange for us to visit Cheyenne Mountain. You know, that's the NORAD facility near Colorado Springs. Radman just called me back."

Frank knew NORAD stood for North American Aerospace Defense, and that Cheyenne Mountain was a large military base. "Let me guess," Frank said. "You think the people at NORAD might be able to tell us about the orange UFO we saw last night, which you think might truly be an alien spacecraft, *and* which you think might be connected to Robinson's disappearance."

"It's worth exploring," Joe insisted. "Radman says we have an appointment at Cheyenne Mountain with a general tomorrow afternoon at two. It's a four-hour drive. You can come or not, but I'm going."

Frank shook his head with amusement. "I'll think about it. In the meantime, how about you and me playing a game? Terry's too good for me."

Joe's game had improved since the night before, and he managed to stay fairly even with Frank.

Terry and Stella sat in the grass while the brothers played. At one point Terry spoke. "Look at all those stars up there; it makes you wonder if we are alone in the universe."

"While you were in with the doctor," Joe said, "I read the pamphlet Sykes gave me. Even if aliens haven't come to earth yet, this pamphlet makes a good case that intelligent life exists out there somewhere."

Joe watched Frank throw his two horseshoes. Both of them landed in the sandbox. Then Joe took his two shots. One of them missed the box, but the other landed closer to the ring than either of Frank's shots.

"Your point," Frank said as he and Joe walked over to retrieve their horseshoes.

"Here's what Sykes has to say," Joe told Terry. "Here on earth, life was able to evolve because of the oxygen and warmth provided by the sun, right?"

"Right," Terry said. "I learned that in freshman biology."

"And the sun is a star just like all those stars we see out there now, right?" Joe said.

"Right," Terry agreed. "It just looks different because it's a lot closer than the rest."

"And astronomers know there are literally trillions of stars in the universe," Joe continued. "Even if only a small percentage of those stars has a solar system, there would still be millions of planets."

"Okay," Terry said with a nod.

"And it stands to reason," Joe said, "that at least a small percentage of these planets, which revolve around suns similar to ours, could support life. And that means there must be thousands of planets with some kind of living organisms."

"I guess," Terry said thoughtfully.

Joe continued. "Then it stands to reason that at least a small percentage of those planets has intelligent life. Like us. In other words, the mathematical probability that intelligent life exists somewhere in the universe is overwhelming!"

"Hmm, you're convincing me," Terry said. "What do you think, Frank?"

Frank got into position for his throws. He had been listening to the conversation with interest. "A lot of scientists say the conditions on earth may be so unique that this is the only place in the universe where life has ever evolved."

"But you have to admit," Joe told Frank, "that there *could* be life somewhere else in the universe?"

"Yes," Frank said, "there could be. But there's still no real evidence of it."

Joe glanced up. By now the sky had turned a deep purple, and the stars were glimmering.

"You know," Joe said, "Frank and I investigate mysteries all the time. But this is really the greatest mystery of all."

"It's also a mystery why I'm not winning this game," Frank remarked. "We're tied."

Frank eventually won the game but only by a narrow margin. Then Frank, Joe, Terry, and Stella went to Terry's room on the second floor of the HQ. They settled in to watch a video Frank had rented in town.

It was a science-fiction movie called *Man from Another Planet*. In the opening scenes, as eerie music played, an alien spacecraft crashed on earth. Only one of the alien crew members survived. "Good pick," Joe said, engrossed by the video.

After a while Stella fell asleep on the bed. "I guess she's seen this one before," Joe joked.

"Or else she finds it silly," Frank said. "If that's the case, I can't say I disagree."

"Personally," Terry said, "this movie is giving me the creeps."

Suddenly Stella lifted her head.

"She knows we were talking about her," Frank said, patting the dog's back.

Stella jumped off the bed and went to the open window. She placed her paws on the sill and looked outside. She began barking.

Terry rushed to the window. "Maybe she's picked up Mr. Robinson's scent. I think that's the kind of bark she makes when she senses he's around. I don't see anything out there, though."

Frank looked out the window. He saw nothing outside but darkness and the empty volleyball court. "There's nothing out there that we can *see*, anyway," he said, "but something has Stella's attention."

"Look!" Joe exclaimed.

Frank turned. The television screen was now buzzing with static. Then a lamp in the room flickered, and the lights went out.

"What in the world is happening?" Terry asked.

Startled voices were heard coming from other rooms. From what they were saying, Frank could tell the electricity had gone out in other rooms, too. Stella continued to bark.

"Shh," Terry said, stroking Stella. "It's all right, sweetie. It's all right."

Joe had a strange look on his face.

"What is it?" Frank asked his brother.

Joe spoke softly. "According to the pamphlet Sykes gave me, aliens often cause electrical interference when they appear. I'm not saying that's what this is, okay? But that's what it might be!"

9 Take Me with You

"We have to check this out," Terry said. She darted from the room, followed by Joe and Stella.

Frank stayed behind, his thoughts turned to Alastair Sykes. If Sykes had kidnapped Robinson to make it look like an alien abduction, maybe he had just tampered with the electricity to heighten the impression that aliens were nearby.

Frank ran down to the lobby and discovered that the lights were still working there. He went to the check-in desk. He found Sykes's number in a phone book and called the number. After two rings, Sykes answered.

"Uh, hi, Mr. Sykes," Frank spoke into the phone. "This is Frank Hardy. My brother and I came by your place earlier today."

"Yes, I remember," Sykes said.

If Sykes was at home, Frank realized, he couldn't have tampered with the electricity. Still, Sykes could have hired someone to do it for him.

Frank decided to feel the man out. "All of a sudden," Frank told Sykes, "some of the electricity at the place where I'm staying is going haywire."

"Really," Sykes said with great interest. "Supposedly that's a common occurrence when Visitors are in the vicinity. Many abductees claim that right before they get abducted their lights flicker or their car engines temporarily die. Some experts speculate that the aliens radiate an electromagnetic field that interferes with the power sources. I should come investigate. Where are you?"

"I'm at the Silver Crest resort," Frank said.

"Wait . . . where?" Sykes said. "I thought I just saw . . ."

Sykes sounded distracted now, as if he had seen something unusual.

"Mr. Sykes, are you there?" Frank said.

"Yes, I'm—I'm here," Sykes said, his voice trembling with alarm. "Uh, Frank, I have to go."

"Are you all right?" Frank asked.

"I think so," Sykes said, "but . . . I really . . . have to go. Good-bye."

Frank heard a click at the other end of the line. He redialed the phone number, but after a few rings an answering machine picked up. "You have reached Alastair—"

Frank hung up the phone. Several people had now come downstairs, puzzled by the power outage on the second floor. Frank ran outside and found Terry, Joe, Stella, and Chris, whom Terry introduced as the resort's handyman, in a storage shed that adjoined the HQ. As Terry held a flashlight, Chris studied an electrical feed box.

"What happened?" Frank asked.

"Loose cable," Chris replied as he studied the wires.

"How could that have happened?" Frank said.

"It could have just happened on its own," Chris said, working with a screwdriver. "Or someone could have fiddled with it. But I don't see why."

"Could a strong electromagnetic field have disturbed the cable?" Joe asked.

"Well, I suppose so," Chris said.

"Joe," Frank said urgently, "do you still have the keys to the Jeep?"

Joe looked confused. "Sure. Why?"

Frank took Joe's arm. "We need to take a drive to Sykes's house. Come on."

As Frank and Joe headed for the Jeep, Frank reported his conversation with Sykes. "I'll drive," Frank said as he hopped into the driver's seat.

Frank maneuvered the Jeep around the curving roads to Sykes's house in just under fifteen minutes. A few lights were on in the house, but there was no answer when Joe buzzed the intercom box.

"Sykes needs our help," Frank said. "This calls for drastic measures." He pulled a metal device from his pocket and set to work picking the lock. After a few minutes he had managed to release the lock. But as soon as he opened the door, an alarm sent out a high-pitched sound.

Frank yelled over the noise. "Look for Sykes while I disconnect this alarm!"

Joe headed down the hallway and stepped through the door that led to the laboratory. The lights and computers were on, and the room was filled with the same static Joe had heard that morning. But there was no sign of Sykes.

The alarm stopped, and Frank entered the lab.

"He's not here," Joe said, "but look at what I found." He pointed to an open window.

"Strange," Frank said. "He has an elaborate security system because he's nervous about his stuff getting stolen. Yet he leaves a window wide open. It doesn't make sense."

"Unless somebody forced him to leave or he was all excited and left in a hurry," Joe said.

Frank rubbed his chin thoughtfully. "He definitely was scared or excited when I last heard him."

Joe moved to one of the computers. Pictures

were scrolling horizontally across the screen. They resembled the simple drawings of a child. Beneath the pictures, mathematical equations scrolled by. Beneath those were words.

"What do you think all this means?" Joe asked.

Frank examined the computer screen. "I think it's the language he was telling us about. The one he uses to communicate, or try to communicate, with ETs. It looks like the language is a combination of images, equations, and words."

Joe studied the screen more closely. The pictures showed a man being greeted by aliens resembling the one in Sykes's living room. As the pictures scrolled by, the man followed the aliens onto a strange vehicle.

Joe looked at the words scrolling by. They read, "Have no alliance with any government but am a seeker of the truth. Please, take me with you. Take me with you. Take me with you."

Joe's blue eyes flickered with excitement. "Sykes told us he sends out the signals when he suspects aliens might be listening. Maybe he had reason to believe they were nearby and so he sent this message. Then maybe they understood his message and took him with them. Just the way he wanted!"

"Get a grip, Joe," Frank said, his eyes on the screen.

"I know, I know," Joe said. "We've found

several people with a motive to get rid of Clay Robinson, and, who knows, there may be people with a motive to get rid of Sykes, too. But what are the odds the same party would be after both men? You couldn't find two people with less in common than Sykes and Robinson."

"So we should just assume they were both abducted by aliens?" Frank asked." That makes a *lot* of sense."

Joe paced the room, thinking. "What happens when aliens abduct someone? I mean, would they leave any signs behind or anything? The tapes!"

Joe walked to the cassettes on the shelf, the ones containing abductee accounts.

"Come on," Frank exclaimed, "we don't have time to listen to a bunch of crazies right now!"

Joe pulled out a tape. "Let's just listen to one. We might learn something that will help us figure out what's going on—and where Sykes is."

Frank grabbed the cassette from Joe and inserted it into the tape player in the cabinet beside the bookshelf. He pressed the play button, and the deep tones of a man's voice filled the room.

"This is Dr. Simon Parker," the voice said, "and this is my fourth session with Emma Friedland. Emma, are you ready to go under hypnosis?"

"Yes, I am, Doctor," a female voice responded.

Impatiently Frank pressed the fast forward button on the tape player. Then he started the tape again. The doctor's voice returned. "You drove for several miles. And then what happened?"

"I'm still on the same road," the female patient replied. "It's completely dark except for my car's headlights. Suddenly I hear my engine sputtering, and then it just dies. Then I see a big blue light appear through the trees. Then, uh . . . then I get real drowsy. I'm conking out. Just like the car. Everything gets blurry, and then it goes dark."

"What is your next memory?" the doctor asked.

"I . . . I don't know," the patient replied.

"Yes, you do," the doctor said.

There was a long pause. Joe felt goose bumps forming on his arm. He saw Frank staring at the tape player.

"I'm, uh . . . lying down," the patient said. "Yes, I'm lying down on a cold metal table. And I'm in a big room, but it's not like any room I've ever seen. It looks like everything is made of crystal or ice. I want to get up and look around, but for some reason I can't move. I'm awake but it's as though I'm paralyzed or . . . oh, no!"

"What's happening?" the doctor asked gently.

"Some kind of creature is standing over me, watching me," the patient said with a trembling voice. "It's gray with very smooth skin and . . . it's got a big head, shaped like a pear or an onion . . . and it has big shiny black eyes. The eyes don't blink. They just stare down at me as if they're seeing through me, and I feel like . . . I don't like this."

"Nothing can harm you now," the doctor said.

"I feel like those eyes are going right through me," the patient said, sounding upset. "They're diving into my mind, reading my thoughts and — no! It's too much! Please! Please make them go away!" She was now screaming.

"It's all right, Emma," the doctor said. "You can stop now. Understand? The session is over!"

Frank pressed a button to stop the tape. "Unless she's the best actress in the world," Joe whispered, "that woman wasn't faking that story."

"Maybe not," Frank said calmly. "But sometimes people recount events under hypnosis they believe to be true, even though the events may not have taken place."

"Well, maybe, but maybe it is true," Joe said.

Then Joe spun around. He felt as if his blood were freezing in his veins. He saw a bright red light spinning outside the window. Could it be some kind of extraterrestrial vehicle? Were the aliens coming for him and Frank? The same aliens who had abducted Robinson and Sykes?

Now even Frank appeared to be concerned as he, too, stared out the window. "What . . . what is this?" he said.

Joe took a troubled breath. "I'm almost afraid to find out!"

10 The Drifter

Shaken, Joe turned away from the window. His eyes fell on the computer screen and again read the words scrolling by: "Take me with you. Take me with you. Take me with you."

An amplified voice spoke from outside. "I want you to come out of there at once!"

The voice sounded familiar. Joe turned back to the window. He realized it was not an alien spaceship. A closer look showed that the red light was rotating on the top of a police car.

Frank leaned out the window. Sergeant Bunt was standing by the car, holding a radio mike in one hand and a pistol in the other.

"It's us," Frank called to Bunt. "Frank and Joe Hardy. We met you last night."

"What are you boys doing here?" Bunt called.

Frank climbed out the window, and Joe followed. The Hardys quickly told Bunt about the electrical problems at Silver Crest and Frank's interrupted phone conversation with Alastair Sykes. Bunt listened intently.

"When you set off that alarm," Bunt said when Frank and Joe had finished, "it sent a signal to a security company. They called me, and I drove right over. I was out near Parnassa, so it took me a while."

Good thing we weren't burglars, Joe thought. We could have stolen the entire contents of the house by now.

"Do you have any idea what could have happened to Mr. Sykes?" Frank asked. "Or do you have any new leads on Mr. Robinson's disappearance?"

Sergeant Bunt screwed up his face. "I tell you fellas, this whole thing has got us stumped. I'm not what you'd call the gullible type, but I'm starting to think that that orange thing really was some sort of alien ship. And that the aliens who came in it are the ones responsible for these two missing men. It's crazy, I know, but nothing else seems to make any sense."

"Okay, what's our next move?" Joe asked Bunt.

"Well, I'll secure the premises," Bunt said.

"Then I'll wake up Sergeant McCown, and we'll drive around to see what we can find. I suggest you boys get inside somewhere and lock the door."

Frank and Joe had no intention of following Bunt's advice, but they were not sure what they should do instead. They climbed into the Jeep and headed back to Silver Crest. As Frank drove, Joe saw someone wandering through a field. It was the young drifter with shaggy blond hair whom the Hardys had seen the previous night. He was wearing the blue-tinted sunglasses.

"It's that guy again," Joe said. "It's kind of funny we saw him right around the location of Robinson's abduction and now we're seeing him around here. Let's have a chat with him."

Frank pulled the Jeep to the side of the road, and the two brothers climbed out. The young man approached, looking at the Hardys through his sunglasses. He nodded his head and said, "Hey, dudes."

"Hey, there," Frank said. "I guess you're just out for another late-night stroll."

"Sure am," the man said. "Are you going to ask if I saw anything strange again?"

"Well, did you?" Joe asked.

"Nope," the drifter said.

"Do you live around here?" Frank asked.

"No, I just wandered into these parts a few

days ago," the man said. "It's nice. I think I might hang around till winter. See how the skiing is."

"Where are you staying?" Frank asked.

"I've got some friends in the area," the man answered. "They live about a half mile down the road from here."

Frank saw his own reflection in the mirrored blue lenses of the sunglasses. He looked the young man over carefully, trying to determine if it might be someone in disguise. Finally he came to the conclusion that the man was what he said he was.

"Okay," Frank told the man. "Thanks a lot."

The drifter gave a wave, and the Hardys walked away. "I wanted to ask why he wears those sunglasses at night," Joe whispered to Frank, "but I figured I'd better not, in case he has some kind of eye problem."

"I was wondering about those glasses myself," Frank said. "But I think they're just part of his cool image. I think he was telling us the truth. We could probably suspect him, but I think he's just your run-of-the-mill ski bum out for a stroll."

"Maybe," Joe said hesitantly, "unless . . ."

"What?" Frank asked.

The Hardys stopped beside the Jeep. By the luminous light of the moon, Joe watched the drifter wandering through the field. "Maybe he's an alien disguised in human form," Joe said.

94

"Just like in the movie we saw. And maybe he's managed to duplicate every human feature except for the eyes."

Frank let out a chuckle. "You're joking, right?"

Joe hesitated. "Yes, I'm joking. At least, I think I'm joking."

The Hardys got into the Jeep, and Frank drove down the road. Joe watched the shadowy shapes of trees pass by for half a mile. "Listen, Frank," he said finally, "I'm not saying that aliens have come to earth and abducted Robinson and Sykes. That's probably not what has happened. But we can't explain their disappearances, and I think we should get all the information we can. Tomorrow I think we should both go to Cheyenne Mountain to investigate further."

"Couldn't we just call?" Frank asked.

"I don't think they do telephone meetings," Joe said with a chuckle. "A high-ranking military official is someone we have to meet face-to-face. That way he'll know we're on the level, and we'll know if he's trying to brush us off with some phony story."

Frank clicked the headlight beams to high. "The closest stars in our galaxy are millions of miles away. Even if aliens could travel at the speed of light, it would take them an incredibly long time to get here."

"Maybe the aliens can travel faster than the speed of light," Joe argued.

"Nice try," Frank said, "but according to the laws of physics, that's impossible."

"According to the physics we *know about*," Joe pointed out. "And besides, you always tell me not to rule out any possibility until it can be positively disproved."

"I can see you're never going to give up," Frank said with a grin. "What time did you say that appointment at Cheyenne Mountain is?"

"All *right*," Joe said. "Two o'clock tomorrow afternoon. Or, as they say in the military, fourteen hundred hours."

By nine on Friday morning, Frank and Joe were heading east in the Jeep, listening to a rock station on the radio. After an hour, they were traveling up the pass that lent its name to the Moondance area. They were on a twenty-mile stretch of highway that wound its way over the Rocky Mountain barricade running down the center of the state. The Jeep was flanked by rising pine trees on one side and a drop down a rocky gorge on the other.

As the Jeep climbed higher, Joe could feel his ears pop from the increasing altitude. Frank leaned forward to see the road better. The highway had just narrowed to a single lane. The road curved so sharply that Frank could see the pavement only several yards ahead.

"There goes our reception," Joe said. The rock

music had turned into static. Joe fiddled with the dial.

Suddenly Joe's eye caught something on the road. "Look out!" he shouted.

Frank saw it, too. Two bikers were hurtling around a curve. They must have seen the Jeep, but they showed no sign of slowing down or clearing the way.

Frank knew it was too late to avoid a collision by slamming on the brakes. He had a split-second decision to make. He could run down the bikers, plow into the side of the mountain, or send the Jeep flying several thousand feet down the mountainside.

No matter what he did, Frank realized, they were in deep trouble.

11 Cheyenne Mountain

A desperate idea came to Frank. He knew it would take a little skill and a lot of luck.

"Hang on!" Frank cried. He jammed his foot on the brake and pulled the steering wheel sharply to the left. Everything was a wild swirl of motion as the Jeep spun in a half-circle. The tires screeched against the asphalt. Any second, Frank knew, the Jeep could plunge over the side of the mountain.

But it didn't. It jolted to a stop—on the wrong side of the road facing in the wrong direction.

Frank and Joe sat a moment in stunned silence, each happy to be in one piece with no dents to the Jeep.

Then Frank leaned out his window to see Bev

and Myra pedaling away and looking back at the Jeep. They both wore big smiles, as if they were more excited than shaken up by the near-accident.

"We heard you coming!" Bev called out. "We just like to wait till the last possible second!"

"Nice maneuvering!" Myra called. "You should pass your driving test with flying colors!"

With that, both bikers picked up speed and disappeared around the bend.

"I don't like those girls," Joe said with a scowl. "I don't like them one bit."

Frank shook his head in disbelief. "They're a menace. I can't believe they were playing chicken with us. Either they're crazy or they don't put much value on human life. I say we check them out when we get back."

The rest of the drive went by without incident. Frank turned off the highway at a sign that read, Cheyenne Mountain Air Station, Authorized Traffic Only.

Frank drove along a paved road for a half-mile or so then came to a guard station, where an armed soldier instructed Frank to leave his vehicle in the nearby parking lot.

After parking the Jeep, Frank and Joe walked to a visitor's center, where they were met by a young airman in uniform. He was expecting them.

"I'll be escorting you inside the Mountain to

see General Webster," he said. "The name's Parker." He saluted Frank and Joe.

Frank realized that Parker was probably only a year or two older than he. Airman Parker escorted the Hardys to a car, then drove them toward a vast mountain that stood about a half-mile away. Frank had heard stories about this place. The NORAD facility was housed deep inside Cheyenne Mountain so it would be able to withstand a nuclear explosion.

At the base of the mountain, the car entered a tunnel and kept going. As lights shone through the darkness, Frank could see that the roof and sides of the tunnel were solid granite.

"The complex is a third of a mile into the Mountain," Parker said. "And the entire complex sits on gigantic shock absorbers. No question, this baby was built to last."

After passing another guard station, their escort parked the car inside the tunnel. He walked the Hardys past a massive open door that contained a series of giant bolts. "That door shuts if we know there's a bomb headed our way," the airman said. "No one gets in and no one gets out until everything is over."

"We should put one of those on our garage," Joe said. He could see the door was nearly three feet thick.

Airman Parker led the Hardys down a polished hallway that reminded Joe of the corridor of a ship. He noticed that some of the doors had small computerized boxes that needed to be programmed correctly in order to gain entry.

It looked to Joe as if a statue was standing at the end of the hall. It turned out to be a man in a gray air force jumpsuit. Everything about the man seemed to stand at attention, including the silver hairs of his crew cut. Joe noticed a general's star on each shoulder.

"I'm General John Webster," the man said, giving both Hardys a firm handshake. "You must be Frank and Joe. General Radman told me that your dad did the Air Force a tremendous favor a short time ago and that I was to roll out the red carpet for you."

Airman Parker was excused, and General Webster escorted the Hardys into a room with a large conference table. An entire wall of the room was made of glass. Frank and Joe could see into the next room.

Suspended from the wall of the next room were a series of giant screens with colored maps of the world. Banks of computers and other technological devices faced the wall and also ran around the room's perimeter. Five men in military garb were at work in the room, all of them wearing serious expressions.

"You're looking at the Command Center," General Webster told Frank and Joe. "All the information coming into the Mountain is processed through here. As I'm sure you know, our main purpose at the Mountain is to detect nuclear bomb threats coming into North America. But we also assist NASA with space missions and keep an eye out for smugglers' airplanes."

"How do you monitor these things?" Frank asked.

"The U.S. has a series of satellites in space that form a circle around the globe," the general said. "Using heat, light, and infrared sensors, these satellites are able to keep watch over the aerospace surrounding the earth and almost every inch of the earth's surface. We pick up this information on computer screens in real time."

On the computer screens Joe noticed live video images of various locations throughout the world. One of them showed a barren desert, another showed a snowy landscape. "Very impressive," Joe said.

"Now, why don't you boys have a seat?" the general said. He sat at the head of the long conference table, and the Hardys sat on either side of him.

"So," Webster said, folding his hands on the table, "what is it you boys want to talk to me about?"

Joe decided to plunge right in. "Your satellites keep a watch on the ground, air, and space of this planet twenty-four hours a day. Have any alien spacecraft ever been detected entering the earth's atmosphere?"

General Webster showed the hint of a smile. "No," he said flatly.

Joe had not traveled two hundred miles to leave it at that. "No, there haven't been any alien spacecraft? Or no, you can't tell us about them?"

The general met Joe's gaze without a blink. "No, there haven't been any."

"Do your computers ever pick up objects that cannot be positively identified?" Frank asked.

"Occasionally," Webster answered.

"Could some of those be alien vehicles?" Joe asked.

General Webster leaned back in his chair. "All right, boys, here's the deal. Fifty years ago the age of UFO sightings began. People were seeing flying saucers everywhere. Naturally the government took an interest and set out to investigate. We found strange meteorological phenomena and a lot of people with wild imaginations, but nothing that remotely resembled an extraterrestrial vehicle. After a while, we decided the work was a waste of time and taxpayer dollars, so we terminated the research."

Joe hesitated a moment, then decided to say what was on his mind. "From what I've read," he said, "the government's investigations were only halfhearted attempts to find the truth."

Webster nodded. "There were people connected to the government who took the research less than seriously. But then there were others who took it very seriously."

Frank felt as if General Webster and Joe were engaged in a game of chess. Frank decided to make a bold move of his own. "There's also some speculation," Frank said, "that the government has made contact with extraterrestrials but is keeping this a secret. Some say the military is analyzing their equipment and is perhaps even communicating with them in order to gain access to their superior technology."

Webster turned his piercing eyes on Frank. "They say we've got some aliens at a secret base in Nevada, don't they?" he said.

"Yes, they do," Frank replied.

Webster scratched an ear and said, "Have you boys ever spent much time with a scientist?"

"Yes, sir," Joe said. "We know a few."

"Well, if the government was interacting with extraterrestrials," Webster continued, "I guarantee we would bring in the best scientific minds in the world. And scientists don't think like military people. They believe knowledge belongs to everyone. And I promise you, sooner or later, one of those scientists would have shared his or her experiences with the world at large."

"Maybe the government wouldn't let such a scientist out of their sight," Joe remarked.

The general turned his eyes on Joe as if he were aiming two missiles. "I know some people think the United States government works that way, but I'm here to tell you it doesn't. The last time I looked, this was still a free country."

The statement hung in the air a moment before Frank broke the silence. "Two nights ago a very strange celestial phenomenon was seen by us and many other people over the Moondance Pass area in the Rocky Mountains. Did your satellites pick it up?"

"Yes, they did," Webster said evenly.

"Do you know what it was?" Joe asked.

"We established it was not a threat," Webster said. "Once we find something is not an instrument of destruction, we usually let it go."

"So you *don't* know what it was?" Joe said.

"No, we don't," Webster admitted. "But I'm a curious man. I saw the readouts on that thing and found the data puzzling. It seems there was an object up there and it was radiating some kind of heat, but it bore no resemblance to any satellites or aircraft I'm familiar with. I sent tapes of the data to a few leading scientists for their evaluation. I'm still waiting for their responses."

"In other words," Joe said, watching Webster carefully, "it's not impossible that that thing was an alien spacecraft?"

Webster gave a faint smile. "Boys," he said, "very few things are truly impossible."

105

The general showed the Hardys around the rest of the Cheyenne Mountain complex, and then Parker was summoned to escort them out of the Mountain. Frank and Joe held off discussing their meeting with Webster until they were back in the Jeep.

"So what do you think?" Frank asked as he steered the Jeep out of the parking lot.

"I got the impression General Webster was telling the truth," Joe said. "At first he seemed to be playing with a couple of schoolboys. But by the end he seemed to be on the level."

"Of course," Frank said, "he could be a good actor. And then there might be limits to what he knows. If information is highly classified, a one-star general might not even know about it."

"Hey," Joe said with surprise, "it sounds like you might be swinging over to the alien-believing team."

"I'm just exploring every possibility," Frank said as he drove the Jeep onto the road. "Just as you suggested."

It was nearly nine o'clock at night when the Hardys hit the last of the winding roads leading back to Moondance Pass. They were just a few miles from Coalville. Darkness made the road even more treacherous, forcing Frank to concentrate on his driving.

Joe had drifted off to sleep. As Frank guided

the Jeep around another curve in the road, he felt a wave of drowsiness himself.

"Ahh!" Frank yelled.

His eyes were suddenly attacked by a bright circle of light. It was much larger than the headlight of any land vehicle. Unable to see anything else, Frank swung to the side of the road and slammed on his brakes.

Joe jumped awake. "What's going on?" he cried. Then he clapped his hands over his eyes to shut out the intense glare.

"I don't know," Frank said, shielding his eyes with his arm. "As soon as I turned the bend, the light just sprang out at me!"

Even with his eyes covered, Frank could sense the white light boring into them. Then Frank felt a quick jab of pain and knew something weird was happening. Frank felt his heartbeat slowing down, and he thought he heard the sound of Joe's voice, but he could not make out the words.

Frank realized he was slipping into unconsciousness and there was nothing he could do about it. The world was turning to blackness.

12 Abduction Number Three

Frank heard and saw nothing. He felt as if he were floating in space, free of the earth's gravitational pull.

Then he felt as if he were falling. He was suddenly terrified that he was about to crash into something and opened his eyes.

His vision was blurred, and his head felt as if it were stuffed with cotton. When Frank shifted in his seat, he groaned. He felt as if his arms and legs were tied to hundred-pound weights. But they weren't. He realized he was merely sitting inside the Jeep.

He had no idea where he had been or what had happened to him.

Frank caught sight of the digital clock on the

dashboard. The time was 10:22. He tried to figure out how long he had been sitting there. He thought it had been about an hour.

Cool air drifted in through the window. Frank waited a few moments, letting the fresh air restore his senses.

Things began coming back to him. He had been driving through the mountains with Joe. He remembered the clock reading 9:03, which meant he had been there almost an hour and a half. Then he had slammed on the brakes when a bright light had blinded his vision.

Wait, he had been driving with Joe!

Frank turned to the passenger seat, then the backseat. There was no sign of Joe.

Frank threw open the door of the Jeep and climbed out. He found himself on the side of the road. The dark shapes of pine trees loomed nearby, and the moon glowed in the sky. But there was no sign of Joe.

"Joe!" Frank shouted. "Can you hear me!"

There was only silence.

Had Joe been kidnapped? Frank thought frantically. But how and why? The whole thing was just too weird. Frank found himself wondering if maybe, just maybe, Joe had been abducted by aliens. Maybe the aliens had made Frank unconscious so he couldn't watch them.

Frank took a deep breath, hoping it would calm him down. If he let his fear get the better of him, he wouldn't be able to figure anything out. Yes, Frank thought, maybe Joe had been taken aboard an alien spacecraft, but it was also possible something not quite so weird had occurred.

Frank got back in the Jeep and began driving. Ten miles later he arrived at Silver Crest and went straight to Terry's room. Frank quickly told Terry what had happened.

"Frank, this is getting really scary," Terry said, sitting down beside Frank on the bed. She handed him a glass of water. "There might have been someone with a motive to go after both Robinson and Sykes, but how would Joe enter this picture? We're talking about three completely unrelated people!"

"I know," Frank said.

"Maybe," Terry suggested, "someone felt Joe was getting too close to the truth about something."

"But I know everything Joe knows," Frank reasoned, "and they didn't take me."

Terry stood up. "All right," she said. "Please don't kill me for saying this, but . . . it's starting to look like this really might be the work of extraterrestrial creatures."

The second Terry said this, a thought came to Frank. "You're right," Frank said. "The vanishings are starting to look like alien abductions to everyone—Sykes, Joe, Sergeant Bunt, you, even

110

myself. Maybe they look a little *too much* like alien abductions."

"I don't understand," Terry said.

Frank closed his eyes to concentrate. In his mind he saw all sorts of pieces that needed to be fitted together. Out the window he heard the cry of a hoot owl. It sounded as if the owl were saying, "Who, who, who?"

"Maybe," Frank told Terry, "these vanishings look like the work of aliens because that's what someone wants us to think. Not to prove aliens exist but for another reason."

"What do you mean?" Terry asked.

"Let's say the other night some person or persons killed or kidnapped Clay Robinson," Frank said. "Then let's say that if that party got nervous they would be found out. Maybe they saw clues being picked up. So they needed a way to throw everyone off the trail."

"Okay," Terry said, "I'm following you."

"In the meantime," Frank continued, "there's all this speculation about UFOs and ETs because of the mysterious orange glow. The guilty party sees a way to use this to his advantage. They kidnap Sykes and then Joe, two people unrelated to each other and unrelated to Robinson, to make it *look* as if aliens are just randomly abducting people."

"Could the guilty party count on the cops

believing aliens are responsible?" Terry wondered.

"That *is* what the police believe!" Frank exclaimed. "You're starting to believe it, too, and I'm an inch away from believing it myself!"

"Good point," Terry said. "These vanishings might really be a brilliant way of covering tracks. So if your theory is right, that takes us back to our original suspects."

Frank nodded. "The two biker girls and Jagowitz. I'm not so sure it's Sykes anymore, unless he wants us to believe he's missing."

"Personally, I don't think Max Jagowitz would be mixed up in this," Terry said. "Bev and Myra I'm not so sure about. Remember, we have a good suspicion that they tampered with that raft. And if they did that to get revenge on Robinson, who knows what else they might have done?"

Frank stood up from the bed, his brown eyes focused with determination. "Settling a score with Robinson is one thing. But hitting me over the head and kidnapping my brother is something else. Come on, let's go see if we can find the infamous Bev and Myra. I've been wanting to talk to them anyway."

Frank left a note for Joe in his cabin, in the hope that Joe would show up. Then Frank and Terry jumped into Terry's car.

Ten minutes later they pulled up in front of the bright red house on Route 47. Bev and Myra were in the front yard, tending to their bikes even though it was ten-thirty. Bev was pumping air into her tires, and Myra was oiling a chain.

Frank and Terry got out of the car. "Well, if it isn't our old friend Terry," Bev said sarcastically.

Myra sneered at Terry and Frank. "You've got no right to be on our property."

Frank had not yet had the pleasure of meeting the short blond Bev and the tall dark Myra face-to-face. Now that he had, he liked them even less than before. He found them to be downright mean and capable of just about anything.

Frank stayed at the edge of the yard, while Terry walked up to the women. "You've got no right to steal things," she said.

Myra gave a dismissive wave. "You can't prove a thing, so why don't you just leave?"

Terry wasn't backing down one inch. "Maybe I can't prove you stole anything," she said. "But maybe I've got some proof that you tampered with one of the Silver Crest rafts. And because that tampering caused an injury to one of our guests, the police are considering it a felony offense."

Frank saw that Terry's strategy was working. Bev and Myra exchanged a quick look, both of them showing a hint of nervousness.

"What's your proof?" Bev asked.

"That's for me and the cops to know," Terry said.

113

"She's bluffing," Myra told Bev.

Terry headed for her car. "Come on, Frank. I feel a sudden urge to visit the police."

"Okay, just wait a second," Bev called out. "If we tell you the truth about everything, once and for all, will you lay off about the raft? We sure didn't mean to hurt anybody."

Frank could see a faint smile on Terry's lips. "Yes," Frank told Bev and Myra. "If we buy the truth you sell us."

Myra picked up a rag and began wiping the grease off her hands. "Robinson wanted all the storage areas at Silver Crest cleaned and organized. It wasn't in our contract to do that, but he said he would pay us extra for it. He told us to do a little bit of the work whenever we had a chance and to keep track of our hours. It was a big job, but over the course of a week, we did it and we did it well."

"But when we gave Robinson our hours," Bev added, "he said it couldn't have taken that long. He thought we were lying, so he paid us only half of what we were owed. We complained that he wasn't being fair, but he refused to budge."

"So," Myra continued, "later that night, we went to his office, figuring we would talk to him some more. He wasn't there, but the office was open and so was the safe. We didn't take any of the money in there, but we did swipe something."

"Only one thing?" Terry said.

"Yes," Myra said. "This."

She lifted a gold chain that was around her neck. Frank and Terry moved in for a closer look at the necklace Myra held out to them.

Several gems were set into a piece of gold shaped like a crescent moon. The gems shone with a pearly luster.

"We took it to a jeweler to have it appraised," Myra said. "The gems are moonstones, which aren't all that valuable. And this is the only thing Bev and I have ever stolen in our entire lives. Cross my heart and hope to die."

"Clay Robinson told me there were several things stolen from his safe," Terry said.

"Then he was lying," Bev said. "He lied to us about our payment, too."

Frank studied the two women. They were confessed thieves, and their stunt on the pass that morning had nearly killed him and Joe. But Frank got the feeling they were telling the truth at that moment.

"Did you kidnap my brother?" he blurted out.

"No," Myra said, tossing her rag to the ground.

"Did you kidnap anyone?" Frank said.

"No," Bev said. "We don't kidnap people."

"Where were you at nine o'clock tonight?" Frank asked.

Bev rolled her eyes. "We were at the Canyon Cafe having dinner. I had pork chops, Myra had stew. Can we go now, Daddy? And will you two stick to your word and keep your mouths shut about those rafts?"

"Yes," Frank said, "but if we find you're lying, we'll be back."

"We look forward to it," Myra said with a sneer.

Frank and Terry returned to the car. Frank watched Bev and Myra put on their helmets and mount their bikes. He saw Myra tuck the necklace back into her shirt. Suddenly he remembered something.

Myra said the necklace was made of moonstones. And yesterday Alastair Sykes had mentioned something about stolen moonstones.

Bev and Myra began pedaling down the road. "Hey, wait," Frank called out the window. "I have to ask you something else!"

"Sorry," Bev called over her shoulder. "We're meeting some people at midnight. Gotta go!"

Bev and Myra picked up speed. Frank kept his eyes on the red reflectors on the backs of their mountain bikes. "Follow them," he told Terry.

"You got it," Terry said. She shifted gears and drove after the two women.

Just as Terry was about to catch up with Bev and Myra, the bikers veered off the road and pedaled through a field peppered with rocks. "Sorry," Terry said, putting on the brakes. "My car won't make it up there."

116

Frank watched the bikers bounce over the rocks. Then he saw someone else riding down the road on a bicycle. The darkness made it difficult to determine who it was.

The new biker looked over at Bev and Myra. Then the biker veered onto the field and pedaled madly after the two fleeing women.

"Who's that?" Terry asked.

Frank noticed that the new biker didn't have a lot of style, but whoever it was made up for it with determination. The biker was catching up with Bev and Myra. Then Frank caught a glimpse of blond hair and realized who the biker was.

"It's Joe!" Frank cried out. "He's back from Pluto or wherever he was!"

13 Missing Time

"Are you sure it's Joe?" Terry asked with disbelief.

"I'd know my crazy brother anywhere," Frank said happily. He leaned out the car window and yelled, "Hey, Joe, what are you doing?"

Joe called over his shoulder, "Right now I'm catching these bikers for you! Be back in a sec!"

Joe pumped his pedals hard, and soon he was alongside Bev and Myra. He reached over and grabbed a bar on Bev's bike, forcing her to stop. Then he jumped off his own bike, pulled Bev off hers, and held her in a headlock.

"Yup, that's Joe, all right," Terry said with a smile.

Frank and Terry jumped out of the car and ran

118

to where Joe was holding Bev. Myra pulled furiously at Joe's arm. In spite of the fact that Joe was wrestling with two wild women, Frank could see that he was just fine.

"What's the idea, you big lug," Myra yelled at Joe.

"You could have injured me!" Bev screamed at Joe.

"That sounds funny coming from you," Joe shouted back. "You and your friend try to cause accidents everywhere you go!"

Terry yanked Myra away from Joe. "Where have you been?" Frank asked his brother.

"I have no idea," Joe said, keeping Bev's head firmly under his arm.

"Could you give me a few more details?" Frank demanded.

"You're not going to believe this," Joe said, "but here goes. About an hour ago I woke up in a cow pasture several miles from here. And Clay Robinson was sitting on the ground beside me. Both of us were okay, but neither of us can remember what happened. We walked to Silver Crest and then called the police. I got the note about where you guys were and biked on over. When I saw you chasing these two darling young ladies, I figured they needed to be stopped."

"Let go of my friend!" Myra yelled as Terry continued holding her back.

119

"Was Alastair Sykes also in that cow pasture?" Frank said.

"No," Joe replied. "I called his place but there was no answer. I left a message on his answering machine for him to call us as soon as he returned."

"Where is Mr. Robinson now?" Terry asked.

"At Silver Crest," Joe said.

"Can you let go of me now?" Bev shouted.

"Tell me something first," Frank told Bev and Myra. "Did you say those were moonstones in that necklace?"

"That's what the jeweler told us," Myra said.

"And you say you stole them from Robinson's safe?" Frank asked.

"That's right," Bev said angrily. "Now tell your brother to let go of my head!"

"Let her go," Frank told Joe.

Joe released Bev, who quickly backed away. "Oh, thank you so much," Bev said in her most sarcastic tone.

"Your brother is cute," Myra told Frank. "Maybe we should have kidnapped him after all. And you're not so bad yourself. See you guys later."

On that note, Bev and Myra mounted their mountain bikes and pedaled off.

"They're so charming," Terry said as she headed back to her car.

After Joe loaded his bike into the car, Terry drove back to Silver Crest. There Terry and the

Hardys found Clay Robinson eating a ham sandwich in the empty mess hall. Stella was sleeping at his feet, obviously happy to have her master back.

Robinson seemed healthy and in good spirits, but Frank was amazed to hear that the man had absolutely no recollection of where he had been the past two days.

"I had just gotten some gas and I was driving along that road to see my lawyer, Wilkins," Robinson said with a puzzled expression. "It was dark and there wasn't a soul around. Then, out of nowhere, a big bright light was shining right at me. Next thing I knew, I felt myself blacking out."

"Exactly what happened to us!" Joe said excitedly. Even though he could not remember anything, Joe was thrilled by even the remote possibility he might have been on an alien spacecraft a few hours earlier.

Frank looked from Robinson to Joe. "And neither of you remembers anything between the time you blacked out and the time you awoke in the pasture. Come on. You must remember something. A word, a voice, a glimpse of a face."

"Nothing," Robinson said. "Not a thing."

"That's how it was with the woman on that tape," Joe pointed out. "She couldn't remember seeing the alien until she was hypnotized. It's like the aliens practice some kind of mind control that wipes out your memory. Sykes said this phenomenon was called 'missing time.'"

"Missing time," Frank said. "Well, a shot of some kind of drug could do the same thing."

Robinson rubbed his beard. "I find it hard to believe I spent the last two days on an alien spacecraft, but I'll be bamboozled if I can think of any other explanation for this."

"ETs or not," Terry told Frank, "this shoots your theory about someone getting rid of Mr. Robinson, then kidnapping Sykes and Joe to make it look like alien abductions."

"I guess it does," Frank agreed. "But there's a variation on that theme. Maybe the guilty party wanted to get rid of Alastair Sykes, not Mr. Robinson. And they made it look like an alien abduction by temporarily kidnapping Joe and Robinson. Taking Robinson first would have been a great way to throw everyone off the trail."

"Well, that's an interesting theory," Robinson said, looking at Frank with renewed interest. "You boys are a regular pair of detectives, aren't you?"

"Oh, not really," Frank said with a faint smile.

"Do you know of anyone who might be out to get Alastair Sykes?" Terry asked Robinson.

"The folks from the mental institution might be interested," Robinson said. "But aside from that, I can't think of anyone."

"Who around here would know some details

about him?" Joe asked. "His personal life, his financial situation, anything? Is Wilkins also his lawyer?"

"I don't think so," Robinson said, pushing his empty plate away. "But that reminds me, I still have to sign those papers for Wilkins. He needs my signature so he can file them by Monday. You know, I'd better get right on that."

"It's past eleven, are you sure it can't wait?" Terry asked.

"No, Wilkins is a night owl. I want them tonight," Robinson said.

"Do you want me to go get them?" Terry asked. "I'll be glad to."

"No, I'll go," Robinson added, getting up from the table. "You three stay here and see if you can solve this thing. But don't knock yourselves out, either. You're all in Moondance Pass to have fun. Besides, we do have a police force that's supposed to handle these matters."

Stella sprang to her feet to follow her master. Robinson scratched the dog's head fondly. "No, Stella, you stay put, honey."

"Here," Frank said, handing Robinson the keys to the Jeep. "You'll need these. We used your Jeep a bit."

"Okey-dokey," Robinson said with a friendly smile. "See you folks."

Joe petted Stella to keep the dog from leaving. Frank watched Robinson walk out of the mess hall. Frank found it funny that a man who had just disappeared into thin air for two days was concerned about legal papers. As Frank sorted through his thoughts, he once again heard a hoot owl crying out.

"Joe," Frank said. "Remember how Sykes made some comment about his house being burglarized once?"

"Yes, I do," Joe replied. "He said that was why he had all the sophisticated security equipment."

"And then he made another comment about some stolen moonstones," Frank said. "When I asked him about it, he said it was nothing. But we both wondered if there might be something to it."

"Aha!" Terry exclaimed. "That's why you were so interested in the fact that Myra's necklace was made of moonstones."

"Do you remember exactly what Sykes said about the moonstones?" Frank asked Joe.

Joe scratched his head, thinking back to the conversation with Sykes. "Let me see. Oh, yeah, he was talking about Clay Robinson. We asked Sykes why Robinson would have been abducted by aliens. He said, maybe because Robinson was driving along a deserted road or because he had red hair or because he stole some moonstones twenty years ago."

Outside Frank heard the sound of the Jeep

starting up. Slowly but surely the pieces were now coming together in Frank's mind.

"That's also what I remember him saying," Frank said.

"But what does it mean?" Joe asked eagerly.

"I'll get there in a second," Frank said. "Terry, did Mr. Robinson mention jewelry among the items he believed were stolen from his safe?"

"Yes, he did," Terry said without hesitation. "He just didn't say what kind of jewelry."

"And, by any chance," Frank said, "do you know if Sykes knew of this theft?"

Terry wrinkled her brow, trying to remember something. "Yes, now that you mention it. One afternoon less than a week ago, Sykes came by while I was cleaning the grounds with some of the others. He said he was considering tightening the security at his house. He asked if there had been any thefts at Silver Crest, and I told him a little about the incident with Robinson's safe."

"Is there a connection to our case?" Joe asked Frank.

The hoot owl stopped its cry, leaving the night suddenly silent.

"You might say there's a connection," Frank said in a quiet tone. "I think I may have just figured the whole thing out."

14 Finding Answers

Terry's eyes were wide with anticipation, and Joe sat on the edge of his seat. Even Stella was staring at Frank as if waiting for an explanation.

"What happened?" Joe asked impatiently. "Do you think I was taken by aliens?"

"Sorry, I don't think so," Frank said.

"Did aliens come to earth?" Terry asked.

"I doubt it," Frank replied.

"Then what happened?" Joe said. He pounded his fist on the table in mock anger. "The suspense is killing me!"

"This is still an unproven theory," Frank said. "But it works out fairly well. Here's what I think might have happened. Terry, you told Joe that twenty years ago Clay Robinson left Moondance

126

Pass to do some land developing in New Mexico. You also said he didn't have much money before then. Well, before he left, I think Robinson stole that moonstone necklace and probably some other things from the Sykes house.

"Now, let's say Robinson sold the stuff he took and used it to help start up his business. But for some reason he held on to the moonstone necklace. That happens sometimes. Often crooks like to hang on to at least one thing they've stolen as a sort of trophy."

"And it's a really cool piece of jewelry," Terry said.

"That's probably why Bev and Myra chose the necklace to steal," Frank said. "I think Bev and Myra were telling the truth when they said that's all they took. But for some reason, Robinson was vague about what was actually taken. Maybe that's because that necklace was the one thing in the world he didn't want anyone to know about. His deepest secret, you might say."

"But how did Sykes find out Robinson had the necklace?" Joe asked.

"Somehow Sykes must have seen it on Bev or Myra," Frank said. "He would have recognized it and asked where they got it. But naturally Bev and Myra wouldn't tell him. Maybe Sykes had always suspected it was Robinson who burglarized his house, or maybe he just went around asking questions everywhere. Anyway, when

Sykes came to Silver Crest, he discovered from Terry that Bev and Myra had stolen some things from Robinson."

"That would have told Sykes for sure that Robinson was the thief," Terry said. "Robinson stole the necklace from the Sykes house, and the girls stole it from Robinson's safe."

"So Sykes confronted Robinson and told him he was going to the police," Joe added.

"I don't think so," Frank said. "It would be difficult to prove anything in court. And the crime was so long ago, it would be difficult getting the police to care about the case in the first place. But maybe Sykes told Robinson he would take this information to the Moondance Pass council."

Joe stood up and began pacing the room. "And they would revoke Robinson's permission to build his condo/hotel complex. They granted him the right to build it because they trusted him. But if they knew Robinson was a thief, even if it was way in the past, they would see the man in a different light. This information would kill Robinson's precious Golden Dream!"

"But why would Sykes tell Robinson he was going to the council?" Terry asked. "Why not just do it?"

"Because maybe Sykes wanted to blackmail Robinson," Frank said. "Maybe he promised to keep his mouth shut if Robinson would hand over some of the large profits he was about to make."

"To fund his research!" Joe exclaimed.

"Exactly," Frank said. "But chances are Robinson didn't want extortion or exposure. His only alternative was somehow to do away with Sykes."

Terry twirled a few strands of her hair. "So he made it look as if there had been three alien abductions to cover the fact that he had done something with Alastair Sykes. Which fits with the theory you were working on earlier."

"Yes," Frank said. "And if my theory is correct, then the question becomes: Where is Alastair Sykes now?"

Joe put his hands on the table and leaned into Frank. "Either he's dead, or Robinson hid him away until he knows what to do with him."

Frank stood up. "And I'm thinking Robinson may be on his way either to skip town or to deal with Sykes right now. A few minutes ago he heard how we were getting close to the truth, which means we need to spring into action fast!"

Frank and Joe left the mess hall and headed into the HQ lobby. "Hey!" Terry called as she followed them out. "Hold your horses."

Both Hardys turned. "Look, you guys have done this detective stuff before, and I guess you know what you're doing," Terry said. "But the Clay Robinson I know isn't such a bad guy, and you'd better be real sure you're right before you go around accusing him of being a thief and maybe something worse!"

As Terry held the Hardys with her eyes, Frank realized she was right. "Call Wilkins," Frank told Terry, "and see if Robinson has gotten there."

Terry went to the check-in desk. The Hardys watched her as she looked up a number, picked up the phone, and carried on a short conversation.

Soon Terry set down the phone and called to the Hardys. "Wilkins said Robinson hasn't come by or called. But he also said those papers should be signed by Monday. Maybe Robinson really is planning to go to the lawyer's house, but he just hasn't gotten there yet."

Joe ran over to the check-in desk. "I've got an idea. Maybe we should talk to someone who knows all about this town. Someone who might know the truth about Alastair Sykes and Clay Robinson. I'm talking about Max Jagowitz."

"Good idea," Frank said.

Joe looked up Jagowitz's phone number, then dialed it. He let the phone ring ten times, but there was no answer. "He must be asleep. And I'm not the least bit surprised he doesn't have an answering machine."

Frank thought for a moment. "Okay, let's do this. Terry, call the police and ask if they'll look for Mr. Robinson. Just tell them to keep an eye on

130

him. Don't give the real reason why, though. Say it's for Robinson's own protection."

"Okay," Terry said.

"After you call the cops," Frank continued, "stay right here and detain Robinson if he comes back. Can I borrow your car, Terry? Joe, write down Jagowitz's address. We're going to pull old man Jagowitz out of bed."

"He's not going to like it," Terry said. "Not one bit."

Wearing red long johns, Max Jagowitz glared as he pointed a Winchester rifle at Frank and Joe. The Hardys had come to his cabin a mile outside of Coalville and banged on his front door.

"It's not enough you steal my potato chips," Jagowitz growled. "Now you got to come waking me up in the middle of the night like a pair of wild mountain men! What do you want this time? The potatoes in my pantry?"

"We're really sorry to bother you," Joe said, "but a man's life may be at stake. We need to ask you a couple of questions about Clay Robinson."

Jagowitz lowered the rifle and beckoned the Hardys to come inside. They entered a kitchen with a black cast-iron stove that looked a century old.

"It's all right, Clara!" Jagowitz called out as he leaned the rifle in a corner. "Keep the bed warm for me!"

131

"All right, Max," a woman's voice called back.

"Robinson can stay disappeared as far as I'm concerned," Jagowitz said, sitting at a table.

"Well, he's resurfaced," Frank said. He and Joe also took seats. "And we think he may be up to something dangerous."

"About twenty years ago," Joe asked, "was there a robbery at the Sykes house?"

Jagowitz leaned back in his chair as his thoughts drifted twenty years back in time. "Sure was. That family had a lot of money back then, and Elsie Sykes, Alastair's mother, had quite a collection of jewelry. One summer when the family was away in Europe someone broke into the house and made off with some of the jewels. Everything was insured, but Elsie was upset all the same. Apparently the jewels had sentimental value.

"They never did figure out who the burglar was. That was the first and last big crime I can remember in Moondance Pass. That is, until you came along and nabbed my potato chips."

"I did *not* steal them," Joe insisted.

Frank didn't want to get back into the potato chip incident right now. "There must have been guesses about the burglar's identity," he remarked.

Jagowitz rubbed his chin thoughtfully. "Some people thought it was a funny fellow used to work down at the post office. But, nah, he didn't look like a thief to me."

"We have reason to believe the thief was Clay Robinson," Joe said. "What do you think of that?"

"Clay's parents were good churchgoing people," Jagowitz said. "I think they're down in Florida now. But I never did like that Robinson kid, even before he started building that monstrosity over near Silver Crest. There was always something scheming about him. It was just an instinct I had, the way my leg always tells me when a big snow is coming."

Joe leaned forward. "Does your leg think he could have pulled that robbery?"

"I wouldn't swear to it in a court of law," Jagowitz said, "but it would make a certain sense. Just a month or two after that robbery, Clay left here and started developing land out in New Mexico. Apparently he had some success. I always wondered where a poor boy like Clay Robinson got the money to get a business like that off the ground. No, it wouldn't surprise me to hear he stole those jewels and fenced them for some start-up money."

Joe ran a hand through his blond hair. In a way Jagowitz was confirming Frank's suspicions, but the proof was still not there. Joe's thoughts were interrupted by the sound of Stella barking.

Back at Silver Crest, the dog had seemed reluctant to be left alone, so the Hardys had brought her along. She was supposed to be waiting in the car, but it sounded as if she had now jumped out and was extremely agitated about something.

"We'd better go," Frank said as he and Joe headed for the door. "Thanks for the help, Mr. Jagowitz."

The Hardys hurried outside to see Stella racing across a field toward a nearby mountain.

"Stella!" Joe called. "Come back here!"

The dog turned briefly to Joe, then continued running. Frank grabbed a flashlight from the car, and the Hardys chased after Stella. "She must have seen or smelled something," Frank called as he ran. "Why else would she jump out of the car?"

Joe spotted a vehicle parked a short distance from the mountain. "That's Robinson's Jeep," Joe said. "Stella is probably barking because she senses Robinson is here!"

In the distance Frank saw someone running toward the base of the mountain. Then the figure seemed to vanish in the darkness. Stella kept barking as she galloped straight for the spot where the figure had disappeared.

Soon the Hardys caught up with Stella, who was standing at the base of the mountain, barking as if she wanted to be let inside. Frank ran his flashlight over the mountain and found a door made of weathered wood. A broken padlock was lying nearby on the ground.

As Joe held on to the struggling Stella, Frank pulled the door open. Frank heard footsteps trampling through a long dark tunnel. "It must be a shaft from an old coal mine," Frank said. "We need to go in there. Don't let Stella come, though. She could get hurt."

Frank stepped into the tunnel.

"Stella, stay!" Joe commanded. The dog obediently sat down.

Joe followed Frank into the tunnel, closing the wooden door after him.

The Hardys moved through the darkened shaft, which sloped gently downward. By the beam of his flashlight, Frank could see that the walls were a mixture of rock, dirt, and a glossy black substance Frank assumed was coal. Here and there the walls were supported by beams of rotting timber, and there was a faint smell of gas in the air.

"I hear him running now," Joe whispered as he followed Frank. Joe heard a thud as if something had been kicked. The sound echoed in the hollowness of the tunnel.

The Hardys picked up their pace, but soon a chunk of something hit Frank on the shoulder. All around there were sounds of shifting and crunching and things falling to the ground.

Frank stopped. "Careful. He must have kicked down one of the support beams."

Then the roof began caving in, pelting Frank and Joe with chunks of dirt, coal, and rock. Dust was filling the air fast, and Joe felt it floating into his eyes and mouth. There was a rumble, and Joe jerked out of the way as a chunk of rock big enough to kill him crashed to the ground.

"It's an avalanche!" Joe cried out. "It's on both sides of us. Either way we go, we get buried alive!"

15 Danger
Underground

"Cover your head and keep going!" Frank called as he held up both arms and trotted down the slope. "If that person was trying to kill us, then there must be something here he doesn't want us to find!"

Joe winced with pain as he was bombarded by hard objects. A jagged piece of rock hit the hand he was holding over his head, but he kept moving down the slope. A spray of dirt flew into Joe's mouth, but he just spit it out.

Soon the avalanche was safely behind the Hardys. They both rubbed the crud from their eyes as they continued down the seemingly endless slope. They had made it over the first hurdle, Frank thought, but what would they find next?

After a few more yards the tunnel opened into a large, cleared area. Frank and Joe stopped, and Frank played his flashlight around the area. The brothers gasped at what they saw.

The beam fell on the face of Clay Robinson. He was standing at the far end of the room, watching the Hardys.

"I see you made it," Robinson said coolly.

Frank moved his flashlight. The beam picked out Alastair Sykes. He was sitting on the ground, his hands tied behind him around one of the timber beams. Sykes looked worn down, as if he had not slept or eaten much in the last day.

"You shouldn't have come," Sykes said wearily. "He'll never let you out of here alive."

"We're taking Sykes with us," Joe declared.

Frank turned the beam on Robinson. "You'll stay right where you are," Robinson said in a low voice. He reached a hand into his pocket, then he pulled out a gold lighter, flicked it, and briefly showed a flame.

"You may have noticed a funny smell in here," Robinson said. "That's methane gas escaping from the coal. This place hasn't been ventilated for decades, and quite a lot of that gas has built up. If I set one of these rotting beams on fire—*kapow*—the whole place explodes. In other words, you'd better not try anything I don't like."

Frank had heard about terrible explosions in coal mines, and he knew Robinson might now be

138

desperate enough to make one happen. If the Hardys got out of here alive, Robinson knew they would have him arrested. But then an explosion would kill Robinson, too. Unless the man had an escape plan.

The beam on Frank's flashlight went out. The room was thrown into darkness.

"Aw, you can never count on these things," Frank said with disgust.

"Stay where you are," Robinson warned.

In the darkness, Frank touched Joe's arm. The Hardys had been working together so long they could communicate in very small ways. Joe knew Frank had put out the light on purpose. Frank would now get Robinson talking, and this would give Joe a chance to creep close enough to grab him.

"You're a good businessman, Mr. Robinson," Frank said. "Too bad you built everything on a foundation of stolen goods. Just one question. Why did you keep the moonstone necklace?"

"I liked it," Robinson answered.

Joe held his breath in the dark.

"That was your big mistake," Sykes said from the ground. "I saw that woman, Myra, in town, leaning over to fix her bike. The necklace was dangling down from her neck, and I got a good look at it. She gave me some story about where she got it, but I could see she was lying."

"And you, Sykes," Frank said, "you tried to

blackmail him, didn't you? If you didn't tell the city council about Robinson being a robber, he would finance your research."

As Frank spoke, Joe took two steps forward.

"Blackmail is a black hole of deceit," Sykes said. "I realize that now. But I knew if I could just get my hands on some more money, I would be able to find out what really lies up there in the stars. What an irony that now I shall end my life here, deep in the bowels of the earth."

Robinson chuckled. "You must be pretty sharp, boys, to have figured all this out."

Joe took another step forward.

Frank detected a hint of pride in Robinson's voice. Most criminals Frank had met liked to boast about their brilliance, and Frank saw this as a good way to keep Robinson talking.

"We are sharp," Frank said. "But your plan was masterful. How did you think of it?"

"Well," Robinson said as if beginning a good story, "after considering Alastair's offer, I decided I wasn't going to give him a nickel. Nor was I going to let him ruin my development project. That meant I had to kill him, but I needed to do it in a way so the crime would never get pinned on me."

"Then an answer came to you from the sky," Frank told Robinson.

"That's right," Robinson said. "When that orange thing appeared and everyone started talking about UFOs, it dawned on me plain as day. I'd read a bit about these alien abductions and right then I told myself, 'Clay ol' boy, tonight those aliens are coming for you.' I brought you boys with me that night so my disappearance would be discovered immediately.

"When I left my Jeep, I came here to the mine and spent the night. The next morning I walked to Parnassa, picked up a paper, and saw Sykes was playing right into my hands, telling everyone that aliens had taken me."

By the time Robinson paused, Joe was halfway across the room. But he knew that the closer he got to Robinson, the more careful he would have to be.

"Then the next night you sneaked onto the grounds at Silver Crest and loosened a cable," Frank said.

Very quietly, Joe took a single step.

"That was just to create a little alien atmosphere," Robinson said boastfully. "Stella knew I was there. I could tell from her bark."

Frank remembered Stella barking out the window that night. "Too bad she can't speak English," Frank said.

"Yes, it is," Robinson agreed. "Anyway, after that I showed up at the Sykes house. I had rented a car by now in Parnassa under a fake name. Sykes was plenty surprised to see me, but then he realized I had probably come to give him his first payoff. Instead I tied him like a hog and took him out the window with me. I figured that would be a more alienlike way of making an exit."

Sykes grunted with disgust.

"But you still needed one more abduction," Frank said.

"That's right," Robinson agreed. "To make the alien story really stick. I set up alongside the road with a big light taken from my construction site and a syringe filled with a substance used for knocking out cattle. I was planning to take the first person who came by, and it just happened to be you boys. After blinding you with the light, I just reached in the window and gave you each a few milligrams from the syringe, and down you both went. Then I threw Joe over my shoulder fireman-style and carried him to that cow pasture."

Robinson was so carried away with his boasting that he hadn't noticed that Joe was now only several feet away.

"You figured it would make perfect sense for the aliens to return you and Joe but keep Sykes," Frank said.

"You got it," Robinson replied.

"But how could you be so sure the cops would buy the abduction theory?" Frank asked.

Robinson let out a laugh. "Because I did the whole thing so beautifully. And because they're not the brightest law enforcement officials in the world. There's just one thing that went wrong."

"What's that?" Frank asked.

Robinson's voice turned somber. "I have to kill three people now instead of one."

Joe lunged through the darkness and grabbed Robinson around the neck. He felt an elbow shoot into his gut, but he didn't let go.

"We're right here!" Joe called to Frank as he tried to wrestle Robinson down. But the man was even stronger than Joe expected. Robinson's elbow shot out again, this time knocking the wind from Joe.

"What's going on?" Sykes called out.

Joe fell to the ground, gasping for air, but Frank was right there, grabbing on to Robinson's right arm and twisting it behind the man's back. Robinson cried out in pain.

Then Robinson threw his body backward and sent Frank crashing into one of the timber beams. Frank's head rang as it hit the wood. Then Robinson pulled himself free.

Frank grabbed his head and tried to focus. He heard Joe getting up from the ground, and he heard Robinson running and then climbing up something. Frank ran for his flashlight and switched it on.

"I'm right here!" Robinson shouted.

Frank aimed the beam at Robinson. He was standing on a second level about fifteen feet high.

There was a wooden ladder there, and Robinson was now in the act of pulling the ladder to his level. Frank had not seen this level or the ladder before.

"There's another opening just a few yards from where I stand," Robinson said, panting from the scuffle. "You won't be able to get to it, though. Nor will you get out the way you came in. At least not before this place turns into a live volcano."

Robinson pulled out his lighter, its gold case glinting in the beam of the flashlight. Robinson opened the case.

"Don't!" Joe yelled.

Robinson flicked the wheel. A flame leapt up.

"Please! No!" Sykes screamed in terror.

"The place will take a minute or so to ignite," Robinson said calmly, moving to a support beam. "I'm going to set this old timber on fire, then beat it before the big bang comes. I want you to know, I don't relish doing this, but it's my only way out."

Robinson held the flame to the wood.

Frank took a breath, telling himself not to panic. "You may be a thief, Mr. Robinson," he called up, "but you're not a killer."

"We'll see about that," Robinson said, watching the flame lick against the wood.

"Why didn't you kill Sykes as soon as you captured him?" Frank said, his voice showing just a touch of the fear he was feeling. "Why did you bring him here and keep him alive for over twenty-four hours? Because deep in your heart, you don't want to kill anyone."

Robinson turned to Frank as he kept the flame on the timber. There was a combination of fear and determination in his voice. "Remember what I told you boys the other night? I said once you've got it into your head to do something, you stick to your guns. Well, the three of you have gotten in the way of my plans, so, by golly, you've got to be destroyed."

The flame had caught the timber on fire.

Just then footsteps were heard entering the room, and Frank swung the flashlight around to find Stella standing nearby. The dog moved her head around as she sniffed the air. Then she picked up her master's scent and looked up at the second level.

She let out two barks as if to say, "Come on, let's get out of here on the double!"

Frank aimed the flashlight back at Robinson. There was anguish on the man's face as he looked down at his beloved dog. "Oh, Stella," he said softly, "you shouldn't have come here."

The flame was spreading on the timber beam. Joe held his breath as he watched, expecting an explosion any second. But he was also remembering what Terry had said about how Stella may have been the only thing Robinson really cared about.

Robinson slammed his hand against the beam, putting out the fire with it.

"Sixteen to fifteen," Joe told Frank. "I am finally winning a game."

The Hardys were playing another game of horseshoes as Terry and Stella sat nearby watching. It was way past midnight, but everyone was too keyed up to think about sleep.

Robinson had been unable to blow up the mine with Stella present, and there was no way he could have gotten Stella out without the Hardys getting him first. To Robinson's credit, he had finally given up. Then Joe had run back to Jagowitz's house to call the police. Soon after, the police had taken Clay Robinson away in handcuffs. Robinson was now in the single cell at the Coalville police station, and Alastair Sykes was safely back at his house.

Joe sent a horseshoe sailing through the air, and it fell around the ring with a loud clang. "Ringer!" he cried triumphantly. "I win!"

"Congratulations," Frank said with a smile.

"Shh," Terry whispered. "It's late."

After collecting the horseshoes, Frank and Joe sat beside Terry and Stella. Everyone else at Silver Crest had turned in, and the night was peacefully quiet. Stella had no way of knowing where her master was, but all the same, Joe thought she looked truly sad.

Terry stroked the dog reassuringly. "You know, I thought of taking Stella back to Bayport with me when the summer ends. But I think she would miss the mountains too much. I'm sure one of the year-round employees here will be happy to have her."

"Anybody would be happy to have this dog," Joe said. "She's as true as they come."

"Unlike Mr. Robinson," Terry said. "I thought he was an okay guy, but was I wrong. Just goes to show, you can never be too sure about some people."

Frank looked in the direction of Robinson's construction site. "Well," he said, "I guess the Golden Dream won't be built after all."

"Maybe it's for the best," Terry said, lying on the ground and looking up at the stars. "Maybe this land wasn't meant to be overrun by tourists and out-of-towners."

"I wouldn't be so sure of that," Joe remarked.

"Why not?" Frank asked.

Joe glanced up at the glittering stars. "There's still not a single good explanation for that orange phenomenon. Think what you want, but I've got a feeling that was a flight from really far out of town!"

"I wonder if they're good at horseshoes," Frank added, then ducked a punch from his younger brother.

THE HARDY BOYS® SERIES By Franklin W. Dixon

NANCY DREW® MYSTERY STORIES By Carolyn Keene

A MINSTREL® BOOK

Published by Pocket Books

Simon & Schuster, Mail Order Dept. HB5, 200 Old Tappan Rd., Old Tappan, N.J. 07675

Please send me copies of the books checked. Please add appropriate local sales tax.

☐ Enclosed full amount per copy with this coupon (Send check or money order only)

☐ If order is $10.00 or more, you may charge to one of the following accounts: ☐ Mastercard   ☐ Visa

Please be sure to include proper postage and handling: 0.95 for first copy; 0.50 for each additional copy ordered.

Name _____

Address _____

City _____   State/Zip _____

Credit Card # _____   Exp.Date _____

Signature _____

Books listed are also available at your bookstore. Prices are subject to change without notice.

760-29